Cocoa and Chanel
Book One In
The Chanel Series

LUSH PUBLICATIONS
PERTH

Acknowledgements

Felicity - thank you for your care, knowledge and many hours correcting my silly mistakes. Thank you also for taking the time to teach me. I enjoyed our coffee sessions immensely.

Mum – thank you for once again reading my manuscript until you could quote it back at me. Most would have given up well before then.

Shannell – thank you for letting me use a character inspired by your sunny, fun-loving nature. I miss you.

Brave men and women of the New South Wales Police Force - thank you for doing your best to keep us safe, and daily laying your lives on the line. I apologise for taking artistic licence with some information I gained during my research. I assure you I have tried to remain as close as possible to fact wherever possible.

None of the characters created in this story in any way shape or form resemble real life people. Except for Chanel, who was inspired by a friend, but that is where the similarity ends. The rest of the novel is pure fiction, flights of fancy and plain old good fun.

Of all the dead bodies I've seen in my life, this one disturbed me the most. It wasn't the vacant eyes, or the ragged cut at her throat. It wasn't the blood pooled in her long blonde hair, or the random senselessness of her death. It was the fact that I knew, somewhere in the dark shadows of the deserted alley, the killer lay in wait.

Chapter One

How Did I Get Myself Into This Mess?

It wasn't my boss that I hated. It was my boss's husband, Lenny - a fat lazy specimen of a man, with overtly frisky hands. Everybody knew Lenny was a perve, everybody that is except Cindy, my boss.

Lenny and Cindy owned Glamor, the prestigious hairdressing salon I worked at. And when I say prestigious, I mean prestigious for Hickery, the small country town I grew up in. We served coffee and our magazines were current. That was as good as it gets in Hickery.

I was in the storeroom sorting out stock when the bell on Glamor's front door jangled. That was the last noise I wanted to hear fifteen minutes before knock-off time on a Friday. With Cindy, the client always came first - which was a nice work ethic, but it sucked when it meant I stayed late. And that Friday night I had plans to meet Becky, my best friend, at Hickery's one and only bar, The Brimstone. I didn't want to be stuck at work trying to guess the exact shade of lilac hair old Mrs Peterson wanted when I could be sharing a bottle of sparkling wine with Becky.

'Cindy?' I called out, crossing my fingers. She had taken the day off to visit her Mum.

The door to the storeroom opened and I groaned inwardly as Lenny leant against the door frame.

'Oh hi,' I said dismissively, hoping Cindy was with him.

'Chanel,' he said, nodding his head at me and attempting to look down my blouse.

I stood up, assessing whether I could make it out the door without having to rub up against his rotund gut. It didn't look good. Between my boobs and his belly there just wasn't enough room for both of us.

'Excuse me,' I said, smiling brightly as I gestured towards the doorway.

He didn't move away, as I'd really hoped he would, but instead lurched further into the cramped storeroom. Leering down at me, he said, 'Nice girl like you should have a man to look after her.'

'I don't need a man to look after me,' I said as I backed away from him. The truth was that I didn't have a man, not because I didn't want one, but because the hot men were a little light on the ground in Hickery. 'And anyway,' I added, 'I've got Cocoa.' Cocoa was the love of my life. A miniature black schnauzer my now ex-boyfriend, Tommy, had given me for my birthday last year.

'That's a dog, not a man. A girl like you needs a real man.' He grabbed his crutch as he uttered the last words and moved even closer.

Oh shit. I was in serious trouble.

'And how lucky Cindy is to have you.' I could smell the stench of his fetid breath tainted with a hint of alcohol. 'By the way where is Cindy?'

'At her Mum's.'

'Great,' I said, squishing myself into the far corner of the room. My mind raced, trying to come up with a suitable plan to get out of my situation which was, in every way, shape and form, bad. To start with, Lenny was my boss's husband. But more importantly, he was an odious specimen of a man. I found him physically repugnant and if I rejected his advances the creep would probably tell Cindy I'd hit on him. If he did that I'd be out job hunting on Monday. As the only other hairdressing shop in town was owned by my ex-boyfriend's mother, and as I had broken his heart and stomped on his soul (her words) I felt that the chances of my gaining employment there were pretty poor. On the other hand if I did sleep with Lenny I would have to go home and slit my wrists, because there was no *way* I was going to be able to live with that memory.

Knee him in the balls and run, my brain advised my body.

I've always been a bit of a chicken and by the time my body had computed the message, reacted with horror at the thought of using violence before finally agreeing with my brain, he was far too close to achieve enough force for an effective impact.

He looked down my blouse and licked his lips, making me regret my bra choice that morning (you never know when Mr Right is going to walk through the front door), and then said, 'So how about it?'

A vision of Lenny taking me against the storeroom shelves flashed through my mind and I froze in horror. Taking my silence as assent, he put one hand on my left breast and squeezed. 'Bet that feels good,' he said.

My knee took on a life of its own jabbing upwards. It missed his groin and bounced off the bottom of his stomach which was hard like a rock, and not in a good way.

I shoved him backwards with both hands and yelled, 'Get off me.' My breast could still feel the imprint of his fingers. I was going to have to get it counselling.

He looked confused, red creeping up his cheeks to his hairline, highlighting the hair plugs that lived there. 'I thought you wanted it,' he said.

'Wanted what?'

'Well, you always wear those short little dresses and .....' he finished the sentence by mimicking big boobs with his hands.

'I have big breasts Lenny,' I said.

He stared at them, eyes glazing over, and then reached out a hand saying, 'Yes you do.'

'That wasn't permission,' I said, slapping his hand away. 'So that's it? I wear a short dress and push-up bra and you think I want to shag you in the storeroom?'

'Would you prefer a hotel?'

I could see I was getting nowhere and changed my tactic without fully thinking it through. 'Anyway it wouldn't be fair on you,' I said, 'what with me leaving and everything.'

'Leaving?'

'Uhuh.' I kept a neutral expression on my face while my brain flitted from excuse to excuse, looking for a plausible one. 'I'm joining the Police Force,' I blurted out. 'So, as you can see this would be totally unacceptable. After all, it is illegal.' I was pretty proud of myself. I'd come up with the perfect alibi to prevent an affair, and I'd done it under extreme pressure. It seemed to have the desired effect because he backed away from me with his hands held high.

'Police Force?' he said doubtfully.

'Just waiting for my enrolment date.'

'Police Force?' he said again.

'Yes, the Police Force.'

'You don't seem like the type to join the Police Force.'

'Why not?'

'Well,' he said slowly, 'you don't look like a dyke.'

I felt like smacking myself in the head. Good one brain – you could have played the lesbian card, but noooo, you had to choose the Police Force.

I pulled myself up straight and said, 'I'm not a dyke, I'm a law abiding citizen just trying to do my part.' I looked at my watch. 'Knock off time.'

I tried to keep skin contact to a minimum as I pushed past him and out of the storeroom.

***

It took a few hours for the extent of my stupidity to become apparent. I was at the Brimstone with Becky - sporting my new Glomesh handbag and Jimmy Choo knockoff shoes I'd bought on eBay – and onto my second glass of wine; checking continuously over my shoulder as I filled her in on the afternoon's near miss.

'So you're joining the Police Force?' she asked in alarm. I love Becky like my own sister, but she's not the sharpest pencil in the pack.

'Of course not,' I said, sipping my bubbly.

'So what's going to happen when you don't leave?'

The words were just out of her mouth and the implication of what she was saying hitting home (all right – so maybe I'm not the sharpest pencil in the pack either) when my phone rang.

'Shit,' I said to Becky looking at the caller I.D., 'it's Cindy.'

'Do you think she knows?'

'That Lenny tried to hit on me? I doubt it.' I put my finger to my lips and then hit the answer button. 'Hello,' I said.

'You should have told me first.' Her voice was angry and hurt.

'Hello,' I said again, stalling for time. I couldn't believe that the bastard had told her.

'Chanel, Chanel, are you there?' Cindy's voice could shred lettuce at a hundred paces.

'Sorry, bad line,' I said, banging my phone a few times for effect. 'Is that better? Now, what should I have told you?' God I really hoped it wasn't that her husband wanted to bang me.

'That you joined the Police Force.'

Oh Shit. 'Well it's not definite,' I said.

'But Lenny told me you were leaving.'

'Ummmm, I haven't got a date yet. I didn't want to tell you till I had one.'

'Chanel, you should know better than that. In this business the more time I have to find someone to replace you the better. I mean do you know how hard it is to find a hairdresser in Hickery?'

I moved the phone as far from my ear as the length of my arm would allow, wincing as her voice whipped into a frenzy. She finally hung up allowing me to get back to Becky.

'So, when are you leaving?' she asked, her blue eyes swimming with tears.

'I'm not,' I said.

'But you have to join the Police Force.'

'No I don't. I'll leave it a few days and say they didn't want any more female police officers and withdrew my offer.'

'Oh.' She looked relieved.

'Yeah, and no one will be any the wiser.' I mean I know it left a lot of questions unanswered – like what I was going to say the next time Lenny hit on me. But I figured I could say I was gay and I'd be safe.

***

I don't believe in fate or any of that hocus-pocus new-age stuff, but when Cocoa and I finally staggered into the kitchen the next morning (I was doing all the staggering) and saw the newspaper sitting there with the headline of the front page blazing - *Not Enough Female Police Officers – Premier Releases Plans to Recruit More* - I did have to wonder if God had taken a personal interest in my future.

'Crap,' I said, picking it up for a better look.

'You could have told me.' My mother was sitting in the lounge-room still in her granny nightie. Cocoa ran over and started wrestling with the end of her fluffy slippers, growling as he tugged and pulled.

'Told you what?' I said. Of course it could have been my hangover, but I was having a real deja vu moment.

'That you were joining the Police Force.'

'Who told you that?'

'Marjory rang.'

Marjory was Cindy's aunt, so perhaps the damage wasn't too bad.

'She heard it from Tommy, who heard it from Nelson, who heard it from Lucy, who was at church this morning when they announced it during morning-prayer. They prayed for your safety and thanked God for sending you into the battle against evil.'

'Jesus,' I said, slumping onto the sofa beside Mum. Cocoa gave up his grip on Mum's right slipper and jumped onto my lap, settling down to groom his front paws.

'Yes, they asked him to protect you as well.'

I put my head in my hands as my headache increased.

'I don't know what you're planning to do with *him*,' she said, pointing at Cocoa.

Considering this was never a real plan, I hadn't put any consideration into what I was going to do with Cocoa. I was just about to confess to Mum when she said, 'Well, I must say I'm proud of you.'

I peered sideways through my fingers to see if she was taking the piss. The pleased, maternal smile, which was rarely on her face when she was talking about me, told me she wasn't. There was no *way* I could confess now.

'You haven't always given me cause to be proud,' she continued, totally ruining the moment. 'I've had my doubts about how you would turn out in the end - what with the police bringing you home from school that day.'

'It was just a couple of eggs, and they didn't press charges.'

'And your addiction to bad boys.'

'My what?'

'Your love of bad boys.'

'What bad boys?' I asked, wishing there were some bad boys in Hickery for me to be addicted to. The baddest arse we had was Johnny the postman, who was regularly pulled over for busting the speed limit; which was pretty impressive considering his bike was a mutant cross between a lawnmower and an electric bicycle. But he had a limp and a stutter and liked to read comic books, so he wasn't really rocking my world.

'I blame the fact that your father left when you were so young,' Mum said.

That sobered me up. 'You said he died,' I said, staring at her.

She had the good grace to look uncomfortable. 'Yes, well, I couldn't very well tell you he ran off with that slut Hilda now could I?'

I had no idea who Hilda was and I was more than a little shocked to find out that my Dad was still alive: scenes of a beautiful reunion playing through my mind like a slow motion movie.

'Still,' she continued, 'I was sad to hear they died in that freak circus accident. I mean no-one deserves to die like that.'

'Freak circus accident?'

'One of the lions got loose.'

It could have been the hangover, it might have been the stress over everyone being so happy that I had joined the Police Force when I hadn't, it may have been the shock of finding out that my father had run off with a slut called Hilda only to be killed by a lion, but it was probably the combination of all three that caused me to burst into tears. Cocoa looked up from his grooming and attempted to lick my face.

'There, there,' said Mum, wrapping her arms around both of us. 'It wasn't the lion that got him. They were trampled to death by the crowd.'

I howled harder for poor Dad and Hilda, and I'm sorry to say, also for myself. I mean what the hell was I to do? I had an addiction to bad boys, a passion for fashion and I was living in Hickery which had neither.

I let Mum make me a nice cup of tea (her words) and some bacon and eggs while I contemplated my woes.

***

That afternoon I was in a queue at the grocery store, my head in the latest *Vogue* magazine and trying desperately not to think about the Police Force, when I became aware that someone behind me was sniffing disdainfully. I glanced sideways, groaning when I saw Ellen, my ex-boss and my ex-boyfriend's mother.

'I must say, I didn't think you had it in you,' she said.

'Had what in me?'

'The guts.'

'Everybody has guts in them Ellen, otherwise we wouldn't be able to digest our food.'

'Don't be a smartass. Believe it or not I'm trying to give you a compliment.'

I didn't believe it but I gave her a good eighty percent of my attention. The other twenty was ogling a photo of a Lisa Ho dress.

'I thought it was all talk – you breaking up with poor Tommy cause you wanted to leave Hickery and he didn't.'

It had been all talk. The guy was as boring as bat shit; there was no way I would have taken him with me.

'But now I find out that not only are you leaving but you're going to join the Police Force.'

She said it almost reverently. *Geez*, what was it with the population of Hickery and their fascination with the police?

'Of course, I don't think you'll make it. I hear the training is quite gruelling.' She gave me a small insincere smile. 'I do hope you don't get accidentally shot by another student or something awful like that.'

The way she said it left me in no doubt that not only did she hope that I did get accidentally shot during training, but that she wished she could be the one to do it.

'Oh, it's so kind of you to be concerned,' I said, smiling sweetly, 'but I'm sure I'll be all right. Give my love to Tommy.' I added the last bit so I could watch her face turn bright red, then I collected my groceries and left.

I chewed it over as I walked home. There were definite advantages to joining the Police Force. I mean what sane, single, straight woman wouldn't want to be surrounded by a sea of men in uniform? And I had always wanted to leave Hickery; I just hadn't found the right reason. Maybe joining the Police Force wasn't such a bad idea. Maybe this was it.

I stood outside the house I had grown up in and had a vision of myself in 20 years' time, still living with Mum, still talking about what an exciting life I was going to lead; waiting for that life to come find me. And then 20 years later again, old and embittered now, still single because I'd never found anyone good enough for me in Hickery. In that moment I realised if I wanted an adventurous life I was going to have to create it.

I decided then and there to go for it. Perhaps it wasn't the life I had dreamed of, but it was a damn site more interesting than where my current one was headed. And besides, it would fix my Lenny problem, and ifit meant never having to see Ellen again, it was worth leaving town.

***

The New South Wales (NSW) Police application form was causing me some difficulties. The first few questions had been easy enough (Name – Chanel Smith, Age – 24, Address – 56 Swallow Crescent, Hickery), but then they had gotten trickier. I mean they wanted to know what colour my hair was. That changed from week to week. I had, on occasion, been known to match the colour of my hair to my shoes and handbag. If I put down one colour now, would I have to be that colour when I went for the official interview?

I decided to come back to that one and continued my way down the form.

Eye colour?
Green
Height?
165cms
(Without my high heels.)
Weight?
60kgs
(In the morning, naked, when I hadn't had pasta the night before.)
Skin type?

What did they mean by that? Did they want to know what season colours matched my skin type? After a brief conversation with Mum – who was a little confused as to why I was filling it out when I'd already been accepted – I wrote olive, and continued down the form.

Religion?

I wasn't sure I believed in God. I mean, present day excluded, he didn't seem to have ever shown any sort of interest in me, and I had considered him with the same indifference. In the end I wrote down Anglican.

Have you ever been convicted of a felony?

I searched my iPhone dictionary for the word felony and then wrote no.

Have you ever bought unsolicited drugs?

My mind twitched nervously away from the small amount of pot Becky and I had bought as teenagers. Surely that didn't count - I hadn't even inhaled. And then of course there were the two Viagra pills I had bought on holidays in Thailand with Becky. She had dared me to do it, and they still sat in the top drawer of my bedside table. Finally concluding there was no possible way they could ever find out about those I wrote no and continued.

Why do you want to join the Police Force?

Well the truth would never do. I tapped my pen against my teeth while I thought about it. Finally writing down – I want to do the best for my country that I can and I feel I can achieve this by becoming a police officer. I was quite proud of the answer.

I returned to the hair colour question and, deciding it wouldn't hurt me to stay the same colour for a little while, wrote blonde. I had been considering some caramel foils, but I figured that would still classify.

After I had mailed it I slouched on the couch while Mum cooked me dinner. Becky was coming around with chocolate and ice-cream to watch movies later on and I was looking forward to telling her about my plans.

Predictably, her blue eyes filled with tears when I told her I had filled out the application form.

'So you're really going?'

'I think so,' I said. I mean there was always a chance they wouldn't accept me.

'I'll miss you.'

'Come with me,' I said. 'Think of the fun we could have.'

She looked for a few seconds as if she were really contemplating it, and then she shook her head.

'Bobby?' I asked.

'He's talking about getting married,' she confirmed.

'What do you want more – babies and marriage, or travel and excitement?'

She smiled at me. I already knew the answer to that. Becky had always been more domesticated than me. She had done most of my home economics assignments at school (all the ones I had passed) and had been dating Bobby since the ninth grade. He was a nice enough boy – a little boring by my standards, but I was sure he would make her a good husband.

'Maybe I won't get in,' I said.

She dashed her arm across her face, mopping up her tears and said, 'I always knew you'd go on without me.'

'It's not like you're dying.'

'You know what I mean. You're not meant for this town. You're bigger than this.'

It made me ponder what it was that everybody else seemed to see in me. Was it a good or bad thing?

'Even if you don't get into the Police Force you'll leave to do something else.'

The thought of not being accepted into the Force made me realise that I really wanted to get in. Apart from the fact that blue was an excellent colour for me, I was craving the excitement the Police Force would bring. Now that I had embraced the idea, the thought of not getting in was totally unacceptable.

***

My phone rang on Monday night, disturbing my contemplation of the state of my toenails. I picked it up without checking the caller identification, expecting it to be Becky; so I was surprised when a male voice said my name.

'Speaking,' I said, shifting the phone up under my chin so I could rifle through my nail-polish bag with one hand and pat Cocoa with the other.

'This is Chanel Smith of 56 Swallow Crescent Hickery?'

'Yes,' I said, holding up a bottle of hot pink polish for Cocoa's approval.

'We have received your application and want to know when you can start?'

'Pardon?'

'You did send in an application to the NSW Police Force?'

'Yes,' I said.

'You haven't changed you mind?'

'Of course not.' I hadn't had time to change it. I had only posted it the day before.

'Excellent.'

'What, that's it? I'm in?'

'Pretty much.'

'Don't I have to do an interview?

'Nope.'

'A fitness test?'

'Your BMI looks good.'

'A psychological evaluation?' I had been reading up on the process on Google and was pretty sure all of that was standard.

'You sound sane to me.'

'Oh. When do you want me to start?'

'How's next Monday?'

I know I had fully embraced the idea of joining, but now that the prospect loomed I found myself back-pedalling. And then I thought of my life here, and how the most exciting thing that would probably happen to me this week was the hot pink polish I was about to apply to my toes, and I found myself saying, 'Of course.'

'That's the spirit,' the man said. 'I'll email you the details and we'll see you on Sunday afternoon at the barracks in Goulburn.'

'Ok.' I was stunned by the sudden turn of events. Cindy was going to kick my butt all the way to Goulburn and back for the short notice, but hey - what else could I do? If I didn't seize the moment, it may never come again.

I heard the click of the recruiter hanging up and felt a huge smile form on my face. I was going to go to Goulburn and I was going to ace the training and I was going to be the best damned police officer I could be. And if I didn't? Well it didn't really matter – because that's what I was going to tell everybody anyway.

***

Cindy had, as predicted, been livid when I'd handed her my four days' notice. The red of her face had reflected in her blonde highlights giving her an evil glow. I had decided at that point it was best to vacate the premises.

I didn't have a lot to pack – just my clothes and shoes, a few photos of home, and at the last minute I stuck the Viagra tablets in the zip pocket of my vanity bag. It wasn't that I wanted to use them; I just didn't want Mum finding them.

I stocked the cupboard with dog food for Cocoa, trying very hard not to think about the fact that I wouldn't see him for the next few months. I was going to miss his fluffy body nestled up against me at night. I knew if I thought about it too much I might change my mind.

And then suddenly it was Sunday morning and time to go. It seemed like half the town had come to wave me off. The locals from The Brimstone had even made a banner wishing me luck – which would have been sweeter if it hadn't said Good Luck Channel.

I hugged Becky and Mum goodbye and pressed Cocoa to my chest, breathing in his doggy scent. Oblivious to anything bad happening, he wiggled around in my arms till he could reach my ponytail, which he promptly began to chew. Before I could cry, I handed him over to Mum and hopped into my old red bomb. Then I backed out of the driveway and headed for Goulburn.

Chapter Two

Oh Well – Here Goes Nothing

Two nano-naps and five coffees later I finally reached Goulburn. The temperature had risen the closer I got and I was sweating profusely when I pulled up in front of the reception building at the Police Academy. Freezing air flowed over me as I entered and I went from toasted to frosted.

'This is the Police Academy isn't it?' I said, smiling brightly at the woman sitting behind the reception desk.

She pushed her glasses down her long nose and stared over them at me. 'It's the School of Police Studies,' she said primly.

'Where you learn to be a policeman?'

I guessed by her lack of any sort of answer that I was correct in my assumptions.

'Hmm – well I'm Chanel Smith.'

'Chanel Smith.' She glanced down at the paperwork in front of her and started shuffling through it. 'Aren't you cold?' she asked, stopping to stare at my bare legs. I noted she was wearing a turtleneck long sleeve sweater.

'Freezing,' I admitted, my teeth starting to chatter. 'It's boiling outside.'

I was wishing that she'd stop staring at my legs and start looking for my paperwork. Finally after what felt like a year but was probably only five minutes, she handed me a folder, a key and some directions to my accommodation.

'Read that tonight,' she advised me, before turning her attention back to the stack of paperwork.

I managed to navigate through the Academy, one hand on the wheel and one on the map. Finally I pulled up in the car park of the building that was to be my home for the next eight months. Throwing my backpack on, I gripped my suitcase in one hand and the folder in the other. I negotiated my way up the stairs and along the corridor till I found my room. Breathing a sigh of relief, I lowered my bag onto the single bed squashed into the corner of the small room. A wardrobe and a desk with a chair were its only friends.

'Hiya.' The squeaky voice gave me such a fright that I banged my head on the wardrobe door. 'Oh sorry, I didn't mean to scare you.'

I turned to view the owner of the shrill tones. A short girl with a big smile stood in the doorway. She was almost as wide as she was tall. I felt a grin twitch the corners of my mouth, partly in response to her own and partly at the thought of her doing an obstacle course. It was going to be interesting.

'I'm Susie,' she said, holding out a hand.

'Chanel.' I grasped her small chubby hand in my own and beckoned her into the room with my other arm. 'So where do you live?' I asked.

'Right next door. Guess we're neighbours hey.'

'Guess we are. Have you been here long?'

'Got here this morning.'

'So have you worked out the lay of the land?' I asked.

'Ooohh,' she said admiringly, 'you already sound like a policewoman.'

I resisted the urge to tell her that she sounded like she had been sucking on a helium balloon.

'I've met a few of the other girls. They all seem nice. Except,' she stopped and looked over her shoulder before whispering, 'except Nastacia.'

'Nastacia?'

'Nasty Nastacia.' A horrified look on her face, she clapped both pudgy hands over her mouth. 'I can't believe I just said that.'

I decided I was going to like Susie. 'So this Nastacia isn't very nice?'

She closed the door and continued in a conspiratorial voice. 'She thinks she's better than the rest of us. Of course she is,' she admitted ruefully.

'How is she better?'

'Well she's going to be a proper policewoman.'

'A *proper* policewoman? What the hell are we going to be?'

Susie giggled before continuing. 'We got in because of the change in policy. I mean I've wanted to be a policewoman my whole life but look at me.' She gestured at her rounded body. 'I was never going to get in.'

'And what about Nasty?'

'She's doing her Bachelor of Policing at the University of Western Sydney.'

'Huh?'

'It's a three year degree. This is her final stage.'

I was perplexed as to why you would do a three year degree when you could do an eight month course and end up with the same job. 'She's dirty that we got in so easily?'

'Uhuh. I better let you unpack,' Susie said, gesturing toward my unopened back pack.

'It's okay,' I said, 'why don't you stay and keep filling me in.'

She perched on the lone chair causing it to groan in protest. I winced, hoping it would withstand her weight. 'Well,' she began, 'there are twenty of us, and then there are another thirty men in our intake; although some of them are more boys then men, especially in comparison with the Riot Squad.'

That got my attention. 'Riot Squad?' I stopped my unpacking and looked at her.

She nodded her head as she giggled, her brown eyes sparkling with mischief. I decided I was going to like her a lot. 'They're training here over the next few months. I saw them at the canteen today.'

'And?'

She fanned herself and pretended to swoon.

'Oh boy,' I said. Riot Squad - I bet there were a lot of bad asses amongst that lot.

My daydreaming was disturbed by Susie letting out a shrill little scream. 'Is that a Louis Vuitton?' she asked, staring longingly into my wardrobe.

'Got it for my 21st,' I said. 'The whole town pitched in.' I plucked it off the shelf and handed it to her, watching in amusement as she ran a finger reverently over the surface. 'The rest are knock-offs,' I admitted, gesturing at the other handbags squished together. I mean really, how did they expect us to fit all our clothing in one teeny little wardrobe. 'I got them in Thailand last year. But don't tell anyone and I'll let you borrow them.'

'Cross my heart,' she said as she placed Louis back in my wardrobe.

'I don't know how I'm going to fit everything in,' I finally admitted ten minutes later. The wardrobe was stuffed and I still had clothes on my bed.

'I don't know where you're going to fit your uniforms,' Susie said.

'Uniforms?' Shit, I hadn't even thought of having to fit uniforms in as well.

'We get them next term.'

'Well it gives me a few weeks to sort it out.'

I compromised by putting my winter clothing in the suitcase under my bed. When it cooled down I could do a clothing swap.

'It's dinner time,' Susie informed me. 'If we hurry we can get a seat near the Riot Squad Boys.'

Not needing any more coaxing than that I followed her out the door. We ran into a few of the other girls on the way down and Susie introduced me to the ones she knew.

The Riot Squad Boys were queued up at the buffet when we entered the dining hall. A hushed silence fell over our group as we paused to appreciate the view. That they were buff was obvious - even from where we were standing. That they were cute was undeniable, but it was the feeling of danger they possessed that attracted me the most. They were like a group of wild animals pretending to be domesticated. I shivered in delight.

We filled our plates and took a table as near to them as was possible with the gaggle of other students already present. 'Who's the one at the head of the table?' I whispered to Susie, trying not to stare.

'That's Rick.'

'Rick.' I rolled the name around my mouth. Delicious.

Rick's muscles bulged delectably with the minor movements created by his eating. With his dark skin and the set of his puppy dog brown eyes I was certain there was some Latin American in his ancestry.

'Next to him are Tom, Mike and John. That's the only names I've got so far.'

'Considering you only got here today that's pretty impressive,' I said.

A tall, blonde woman entered the mess and strode over to the buffet table. Susie flicked her head in her direction and screwed up her face.

'Nasty?' I guessed.

She nodded her head. The woman took a seat at a table near us and speared a piece of broccoli with her fork. She didn't seem at all interested in the riot squad. I waited for her to glance in our direction so I could smile - no need to get off on the wrong footing if I could help it, but she finished her meal without so much as one look and then disappeared as quickly as she had arrived.

The boys left far too quickly as well, leaving us to eat our dessert by ourselves.

'So what happens tomorrow?' I asked. I hadn't had time to read my information yet.

'Parade at seven,' Linda, a tall red head, said.

We were meant to wear office attire for the first few months so I had come well prepared. I inspected myself the next morning, smoothing down my black skirt, admiring the way it set off my red high heels.

There was already a group of students clustered near the edge of the parade ground when I turned up. I joined them, looking around for the girls from the night before.

Before I could find them a man in uniform marched towards us from the other side of the parade. He was big, in a tall, solid way, and sported a bristling moustache. 'Well don't just stand there,' he yelled, his moustache quivering, 'form up.'

We staggered onto the bitumen and made two lines.

'You look like a group of lost hikers,' he bellowed. 'Form up, 10 abreast, five deep.'

I rushed to the back of the pack - quite a feat in my high heels - and was standing there feeling smug when the students in front peeled away like some sort of organised bomb burst, regrouping behind me until I was standing smack bang in the middle of the front row.

Bugger. The man walked up and down in front of us, ominously slapping a short stick into one hand.

'I've seen packs of monkeys form up faster than you lot,' he growled. 'From now on you will form up in the same order, every day until training has finished.'

'Even weekends?' I blurted out before I could stop myself.

'Miss...' He stared at me, smacking his stick into his left hand more and more vigorously until I realised what he was after.

'Smith,' I supplied.

'Miss Smith, you will form up here every morning, in rain, hail and snow, until I tell you you can stop.'

It snowed in Goulburn? Good grief, I was going to have to get some fur-lined boots.

He turned his attention back to the group. 'I am Sergeant Moores. I will be your training sergeant for the duration of your stay here. If I say jump, you will jump. Do I make myself clear?'

'Yes, Sergeant,' Nastacia said in a militant voice.

'Do I make myself clear?' he asked louder.

'Yes Sergeant,' the rest of us echoed.

He went on for about half an hour, advising us what he expected of us as police officers in training – parade every morning, room inspections and marching practice. I breathed a sigh of relief when he finally said, 'dismissed.' But then he added, 'Miss Smith come here.'

The rest of the students fled the parade ground heading for our first class, while I hobbled over to him. I hadn't expected to have to stand for so long in my killer heels.

'What are you wearing?' he said.

'Office attire Sergeant.'

'That's not office attire,' he snarled, pointing his stick at me. 'You look like you've gone under cover in the red light district.'

I would have been pretty offended if I hadn't seen all the *Police Academy* movies. I knew what he was up to with all his blustering and wielding of the blunt weapon; he was trying to break my spirit.

'What would you prefer me to wear Sergeant?' I asked, glancing nervously at his stick. Was it legal for him to use that thing on me? I was going to have to read my information pack.

'Pants and sensible shoes.'

'Aye aye Sergeant.' I gave him one of my friendliest smile.

He didn't return it. Instead, one of his eyes twitched a few times as he scowled at me and his face started to turn red.

A vast amount of experience has taught me that when people's faces go red they're normally about to start screaming at me. I tried to think of a way to stop the imminent onslaught but there was nowhere to go from my aye aye comment. So instead I braced, as if in a gale force wind, and waited. He let out a low growl, his moustache bristling with the movement of his mouth, and I noticed something yellow - egg yolk? – matted into the hair.

I know I wouldn't want to walk around all day with food on my face and everybody sniggering behind my back so I said, 'You've got some food in your moustache.' I pointed to the left side of my mouth hoping he would realise I meant his right not his left. That can get pretty confusing.

His eye twitched harder as his lips worked around words that didn't make it out of his mouth. I was starting to wonder if he was having an epileptic episode when he snarled, 'Get to class Miss Smith.' He had an impressive ability to make my name sound like a rude word.

The rest of the day passed uneventfully apart from when I fell asleep after lunch during a documentary on the history of the Police Force, and the trainer humiliated me in front of the group. I mean seriously, I defy anyone to stay awake through an hour of that drivel, especially with a full stomach.

The next day I wore black pants and flat shoes. Sergeant Moores made some snide comments about the shoes but the boys, who seemed to have two left feet, preoccupied most of his wrath with their inability to stay in step during marching practice.

After lunch we had physical education. I wasn't looking forward to it at all, but at least I wasn't dreading it like Susie. Nastacia was stretching when we showed up at the gym. I watched her for a while and then started to copy her, hoping I looked like I knew what I was doing. Susie joined me, leaning as far forwards as her stomach would allow, stretching her fingers optimistically towards the ground.

Nastacia looked over and rolled her eyes. 'I don't know why you're bothering,' she said.

'I don't want to pull a muscle,' Susie replied.

'The only muscle you're ever going to pull is your tongue.'

I walked over to her and said, 'That's not very nice.'

'I don't know why you're bothering either,' she said, eyeing me up and down. 'Why don't you just go home and look pretty.'

'Pardon? What's that supposed to mean?'

'It's obvious all you care about is how you look.'

'That's not true at all,' I said. It wasn't. I cared about a lot of things: my Mum, Cocoa, world peace.

'So why do you want to be a police officer?'

'To make the world a better place.' I'd said it so many times I was almost starting to believe it.

Nastacia obviously didn't buy it. She snorted and turned her back on me and continued her stretching.

'All right Miss Smarty Pants,' I said, 'why do you want to be a police officer?'

She stopped and looked at me with steel grey eyes. 'You wouldn't understand.'

'Try me,' I said, instead of my preferable alternative of 'bite me'.

'My father was a police officer, as was his father, and his father before that.'

'So…. it's a family tradition?'

'I knew you wouldn't understand.'

'What's there to understand? You're trying to make them proud of you. I don't see how that is any better than our reasons for being here.'

She shot me a venomous look, but before she could retort someone called us into the gym. That someone was riot squad Rick. *Hmmm*, maybe this physical education wasn't going to be so bad after all.

An hour later I lay on the ground, sweating and panting and wishing Rick had gotten me to this state using a totally different form of exercise. It was official. P.E. sucked big time. The only person more unfit than me was Susie. She'd thrown up half an hour in and been sent to the first aid section for rehydration. Nasty had breezed through the one hour torture session with a smirk on her face.

The only positive thing about the whole experience had been watching Rick demonstrate the exercises for us. That man was a serious chunk of hunk.

***

Susie was looking better when I caught up with her after class, but she seemed glum. I tried to cheer her up through dinner by telling her how disgracefully I had performed for the last half of the exercise program.

'What's up?' I finally asked when we were sitting on my bed after dinner.

A lone tear rolled down her plump cheek. 'I'm never going to be a policewoman.'

'Of course you are,' I said. 'In eight months.'

'No,' she shook her head, 'they'll fail me.'

'You can fail?'

She smiled sadly. 'Of course we can dummy.'

It was a sobering thought. 'Well you still haven't told me why you're going to fail.'

'I'll never pass the physical exam.'

'There's a physical exam?' Well that bit of news had balls on it.

She shook her head and said, 'Oh Chanel, did you read the course information at all?'

I shifted uncomfortably. 'I started to, but I fell asleep.'

She chuckled. 'Chanel, why *do* you want to be a police officer?'

I was about to rote my standard answer of making the world a better place but I stopped. I liked Susie and I didn't want to lie to her, so I told her the truth, about Lenny and Hickery.

She sighed wistfully when I had finished and said, 'What are we going to do?

'We are going to train.'

'Really?'

'Yup. After dinner. We'll go to the gym and work out.'

She sat upright with a hopeful look on her face. 'We could, couldn't we.'

'I promise,' I said, putting my hand on my heart, 'that I will get you through your physical.' The words were out of my mouth before my brain had time to edit them.

'Do you? Do you really promise?'

'Of course,' I said, looking down to see if my nose had gotten bigger.

God I hoped I wasn't telling a porky. As things stood unless the physical exam consisted of a fast food crawl followed by a movie marathon she was going to fail. I would do my best to help her, I really would, but there's only so much a barely five foot munchkin was capable of. If we were required to do something ridiculous like climb over a three metre wall we were going to need divine help. I just hoped Susie's hotline to heaven worked better than mine.

Chapter Three

Lucky Schmucky

After the first week at the Academy our training fell into a rhythm. Parade, lessons, lunch, more lessons then P.E. After dinner Susie and I went to the gym and tried to train. The problem was neither of us had ever worked out before so we weren't sure what we were doing. But after the first couple of weeks Susie stopped throwing up during P.E. so I figured we were doing something right.

I had two big problems - Sergeant Moores and Nasty Nastacia. (Well three if you considered not being able to get Riot Squad Rick alone a problem.)

Sergeant Moores was just doing his job – I think. As I'd never been exposed to bastardisation before I wasn't sure what was acceptable and what was not. I couldn't do anything right. Even my ugly shoes became too fancy for him and I resented the money I had to spend on ones that could only be described as homely.

During room inspection my room was too dirty, untidy or dusty. My clothes were too crushed, too short, too tight. After a few weeks it began to wear me down. My theory that he was just doing his job was flawed by the fact that he didn't pick on the others with the same level of ferocity. It was becoming obvious that I should never have mentioned the egg yolk.

And Nasty? Well the name said it all. Mostly she just smirked as Sergeant Moores picked on me or made snide comments when I spoke. But a few things happened that made me suspicious that she was sneakier than she looked.

Firstly, three spiders found their way into my room. I've never been a fan of spiders. And that's probably the understatement of the year. I once sat on my bed for two hours waiting for Mum to come home from the shops to save me from a hair ball I'd thought was a Daddy-long-legs. You can imagine how excited I was to have three of the little darlings in my room. And these weren't your ordinary garden variety of spider. These were huge with visible fangs, and they were hairy. I'm not sure what it is about the hair that makes them extra creepy. I mean, I've dated a few hairy men in my time and that didn't seem to bother me, but when it's hair on a spider, all bets are off.

I noticed them lurking near my door as they decided which part of my room they were going to inhabit. Given they had cut off my escape route I did the only thing possible. I stood on the bed and screamed until help (Susie brandishing a broom) showed up. I had no proof but I was pretty sure Nasty had been instrumental in the spiders' choice of which door to crawl under. I had seen her lurking in the corridor when I had gone to the toilet, and it seemed a little coincidental that there were three of them. I mean since when did spiders start travelling in packs?

And then a pen appeared in my bag with its end missing and emptied its ink all over my study books. Initially I thought it was my own stupid fault but the pen's hot pink logo had the outline of a topless woman and the words 'We want you to come inside'. I know there was no way I put that pen in my bag. I would remember a pen like that.

But the sneakiest, the lowest, the most damning of them all was the pair of men's undies that was shoved into the bottom of my wardrobe. If I had spent more time tidying up before room inspection I may have noticed them. But I didn't, so it was a huge shock to me when Sergeant Moores dragged them out on the end of his stick and waved them in my face.

It was against Academy rules to have persons of the opposite sex in our rooms, so I stood there staring straight ahead, while Sergeant Moores yelled till his head resembled a giant, saliva flecked tomato. More embarrassing though, I was summoned for an interview with the head of the Base, Superintendent Wolfe. Now *that* was an interesting conversation. I am sure that Nasty thought she had seen the last of me, but I managed to convince him that I wore men's underwear to prevent chaffing, and it all went away after that.

It certainly wasn't a high moment in my life, and between that and Sergeant Moores' bullying I found myself questioning my urge to join the Police Force. I mean, why was I trying so damned hard when it was evident I wasn't wanted?

I was in silent contemplation, lying on my bed in the few minutes before lunch officially started, when I was once again summoned to Superintendent Wolfe's office.

'For goodness sake,' I grumbled to Susie as I climbed off the bed, 'I wonder what I've done this time.'

I could tell by the look on her face that she was worried. I, however, was getting to the point where I didn't give a damn. I think that was what had Susie so worried.

'You promised to get me through the physical,' she whispered as I opened the door.

I stopped and sighed. 'Don't worry. I'll behave myself,' I finally said.

I childishly dragged my feet all the way to his office, but I still got there way too soon for my liking. His assistant told me to have a seat and asked me in a kind voice if I wanted anything.

Oh Boy. The assistant was being sweet. That's it, I was a goner!

I sat and stewed and tried to work out on what grounds they would kick me out. I was doing well in my exams. Maybe I wasn't the most coordinated when it came to marching, but I was exercising and studying hard, and trying hard to clean my room enough to satisfy Sergeant Moores - something I had begun to suspect was impossible. I didn't know what else I could do to make them happy. I sighed. Maybe it wasn't meant to be.

By the time Superintendent Wolfe finally called me into his office I had already mentally dealt with being kicked out of the Academy and moved on to deciding what I was going to do with my life. I was having trouble with that part.

He sat me down across from him and apologised for keeping me waiting. Why was he being so nice? Was he trying to let me down gently?

'I have some bad news my dear,' he said.

I sighed.

'It's your mother.'

'My mother?' I stood up in surprise.

He gestured for me to sit back down. 'Don't be alarmed. She's fine.'

'Fine?'

'In a stable condition.'

Now I *was* scared. 'What happened?'

'She was mugged on her way home from work and broke her leg.'

'They beat her up?'

'No. She chased the perpetrator and was hit by a car.'

Christ. My mother had been hit by a car. I felt sick.

'Seeing as this weekend is a long weekend I thought you could have a few days off to go and visit her.'

I was still too stunned to speak.

'Chanel, are you all right?'

'I think I'm in shock,' I said. My mother mugged in Hickery? The town was so quiet it almost didn't need a police station. 'When can I leave?'

'Right away.'

'Thank you,' I said, standing.

'Oh and Chanel,' I paused in the doorway and turned back to look at him, 'she's still in hospital. Sounds like she will be for a while.'

I threw some clothes into a bag and with Susie's, 'Drive safely,' in my ears I headed for my car. I had been tempted to pack all my stuff and not come back, but Susie had been watching me like a hawk.

The temperature in Goulburn had plummeted in the last week and it wasn't till I opened the door to the chilly air that I realised I had left my coat in my room. I debated not taking it, but the heater in my car didn't work very well, and I was going to need it. I placed my bag in the car and went back up to my room for my coat.

Everyone had gone to the mess for lunch and the building was eerily empty. If it hadn't been, I probably wouldn't have heard the whispered voices coming from Nastacia's room through the slightly ajar door.

'I love you.'

'I love you too.'

I froze, fascinated by the conversation. Nasty in love?

The speaking stopped for a while and I could just make out the sound of skin moving on skin. A low moan and then the kiss broke off.

'I have to go.'

Shit. I was standing right outside the door.

'I know. When will I see you again?'

I started to walk towards my room, but the door pulled opened a fraction more and all of a sudden I was staring right into Nastacia's grey eyes. I saw them widen in horror. She froze in the doorway, but the person behind her, not realising their danger, reached out and pulled open the door.

I don't know which part shocked me more. That Nasty was in love, or that she was in love with another woman? Of course as soon as I saw the brunette, her large green eyes and her perfect red lips both rounded in shock at the sight of me, several things clicked into place. *That* was why Nastacia never joined us in our perving on the Riot Squad Boys. *That* was why she kept to herself. Poor thing – I bet being gay didn't fit into her family's traditional plans for her.

The drive home seemed a lot shorter than it had getting to Goulburn; mostly because I had a lot to think about. I was worried about my future, I was worried about what form Nastacia's payback would take (a plague of rodents?), but mostly I was worried about Mum. And then I remembered Cocoa. *Ah crap.* Who was going to look after Cocoa while Mum was in hospital? My only friend that lived in Hickery was Becky and her landlord had prohibited animals after her Shetland pony had eaten the kitchen. All my other school friends were from surrounding towns, none of those towns being big enough to warrant their own school, and to be honest I hadn't stayed in contact with them over the last few years. I tried not to think about it and concentrated instead on staying awake while I drove.

When I got to Hickery I went straight to the hospital. My attempt to arrive before visiting hours were finished was vindicated when I pulled up in the parking lot at 6.30pm. If I was lucky I'd be able to steal Mum's jelly.

I don't know what I'd been expecting but I was relieved when I entered the room and saw her sitting up in bed. Sure, her leg looked a little scary; its cast suspended by ropes from the bed frame, but apart from that, she appeared to be in one piece.

'You're okay,' I said, giving her a hug.

'What do you call that? Chopped liver?' she said, gesturing at her leg.

'Sorry, it's very impressive. I mean apart from that you're okay.'

We paused while a nurse brought her dinner in. Tough roast beef and over cooked vegetables. Yummy.

'I was lucky,' she continued.

'How was getting hit by a car lucky?'

'The man who mugged me was carrying a gun.'

Icy chills ran over me at her words. *A gun?* I shivered and reached for her jelly. She slapped my hand and moved the little container to the far side of the plastic tray.

'Why did you chase him?' I asked.

'He took my handbag.'

I would have chased him too; *especially* if he'd stolen my Louis Vuitton. It's not that people didn't have guns in Hickery, they did. Shooting was a favourite pastime for some. But they shot foxes, rabbits and pigs – not people. And their guns weren't the sort you could hide in your pocket.

'So they got him?'

'The car hit both of us. I survived.'

'He's dead?' It seemed totally surreal.

She nodded as she peeled the top off her jelly. I sighed and sat back in the seat. Guess I was going to have to fend for myself in the food department.

'Who was he?' I asked.

'Who was who?'

'Did you hit your head as well? The mugger.'

She licked the jelly spoon clean and lay back into her pillows. 'They don't know. He didn't have any identification on him.'

'Hopefully his finger prints will I.D. him.'

'Oooh,' she said, 'listen to you - quite the little policewoman. How's the training going?'

I contemplated telling her about Sergeant Moores and Nastacia but as the sentences were forming in my head I realised how lame they sounded.

Looking at her, lying under the crisp white sheets, her leg hovering above her, made me want to get through training even more. If I could stop just one mugger from hurting someone like my Mum then I *was* making the world a better place. All those times I had told that lie, only to realise now I had been telling the truth. For the first time in my life I knew what I wanted. I did want to make the world a better place. I did want to try for world peace. And I wanted to be a policewoman. The rest would sort itself out.

***

Cocoa was as excited to see me as I was him. I pressed his soft body to my chest and breathed in his doggy scent. Then we rumbled on the floor for a while, wrestling and tug-o'-warring, before settling down on the couch to watch television and await the arrival of our pizza.

I had rung Becky as soon as I got home but she hadn't answered. I was tempted to run down to The Brimstone to see if she and Bobby were there but I didn't feel like answering questions about Mum or my training. I had spoken to her the week before and she'd sounded stressed. She and Bobby had finally announced their engagement and already they were having trouble with the relatives. Both sets of parents wanted to host the wedding on their own farm. Plus his mother didn't like her mother and the rivalry between the two was just warming up. I felt sorry for her and wished I could help in some way but all I could do was be there to listen.

Mum was much the same the next morning. We tossed around possibilities for people who could look after Cocoa but couldn't come up with anybody. They were either on holidays, had allergies or phobias, weren't allowed animals, or didn't like me. I was going to have to beg Becky to stay at Mum's for the few weeks she needed to stay in hospital.

Bobby's 4WD was in the driveway when I pulled up outside their house. I could see Becky coming out the door, a bag in her arms. She manoeuvred it awkwardly into the back of the car before she noticed me walking up the driveway. I had expected her to be excited to see me – she wasn't.

'Chanel,' she said awkwardly, 'what are you doing here?'

'Hi yourself,' I said. 'I'm visiting Mum.'

'Oh…how is she?'

I was surprised Becky hadn't been to visit her. 'In pretty good spirits considering her leg is broken.'

She winced sympathetically and then shot an anxious look over her shoulder towards the road.

'Is this a bad time?' I asked. It felt weird saying it. Becky and I didn't have bad times. We were always happy to see each other.

'Of course not.' Her words and voice were at odds with each other.

'Becky what's going on? You're starting to freak me out.'

She wiped her hands nervously on her pants and then beckoned me into the house, checking the road again before she shut the door.

'I'm not going to find Bobby's dead body in the kitchen am I?' I said.

She snorted in amusement. 'No.'

'In the bedroom?' I asked.

'Of course not.'

'Ahh, he's in that bag in the car.'

She smiled. 'Like I'd be able to lift him.'

'People have been known to have amazing strength when they need it the most.'

'Bobby's fine,' she said. 'Well actually he's better than fine.' A grin broke through the stressed look on her face. 'The thing is, well what with all the dramas we were having with the families....'

'Yes.'

'Well, we sort of got married this morning.'

'Sort of got married?' I tried to keep my voice level, but I heard it climb up an octave.

She grimaced as she said, 'Okay, we got married.'

A part of me was devastated that I hadn't been there; hadn't been her maid of honour like we'd promised each other in primary school. But I managed to push it aside. Tears welled in my eyes as I reached out for her.

'I'm sorry,' she said as she hugged me.

'Don't be. I'm crying because I'm happy for you,' I said, wiping my face with my arm.

'Really, you're not mad?'

'I would be lying if I said I wasn't disappointed I hadn't been there. But I'm not mad.'

She let out a huge sigh. 'I've been so worried,' she admitted.

'Geez, don't worry about me. What on earth are you going to tell your parents?'

Bobby entered the kitchen as I was speaking. 'We aren't planning on telling them,' he said.

'Huh?'

'The grapevine in this town works just fine. They'll find out without us telling them.'

'Ouch,' I said.

Becky crossed to Bobby's side and put her arms around him. 'You caught us packing for our honeymoon. We're trying to get out of town before the hysteria starts.'

'We're hoping they'll have time to reflect on their actions that drove us to this before we get back,' Bobby added.

'Good luck with that,' I said, thinking about how upset Becky's Mum had gotten when we'd bought Becky's formal dress without her.

I helped them pack the car and then waved them off on their round Australia trip. They wouldn't be home for months. I didn't bother mentioning my dilemma with Cocoa. It was my problem not theirs and it was just one more thing Becky would have felt guilty about.

***

'What about a kennel?' Mum said the next morning. I was leaving in only a few hours and we still hadn't solved our problem.

'That's a great idea,' I said. 'Except...'

'Except what?'

'Well the only kennel near Hickery got closed down for cruelty to animals last year.'

'Oh that's right, it did too.'

It had been a huge scandal.

'However,' I said, thinking furiously, 'I could take him with me and put him in a kennel in Goulburn.' That would be nice. I'd get to visit him.

And so it was that Cocoa was riding shotgun when I left for the Police Academy. I was planning on hiding him in my room until I got him into a kennel. We drove the whole way only stopping once for a toilet break and pizza - I had Hawaiian, Cocoa had meat lovers – and made it back to Goulburn in record time.

'Don't make a sound,' I warned him as I zipped up the small backpack I used for smuggling him places dogs weren't allowed. I breathed a sigh of relief when we made it up to my room without running into anyone who wanted to chat. He seemed pretty impressed with my quarters, sniffing the perimeter before settling down on my bed.

It wasn't long before I heard knocking on my door. I opened it a little to check it was Susie before I let her in.

'He's so cute,' she said in her shrill little voice when she saw Cocoa. 'How's your mother?'

'Good,' I said. 'But I have to book Cocoa into a kennel until she's out. Do you know if there is any nearby?'

She pulled out her phone. 'No, but I can Google it for you.'

'Well while you do that I'm going to see if I can find Rick.'

She looked at me with her eyebrows raised.

'I'm going to ask him to train us in the evenings.'

'Do you think he will?' Her voice got even higher when she was excited.

I hitched my boobs up in my bra and applied a coat of coraliscious gloss to my lips. 'I'm hoping to put it in a way that he won't be able to resist,' I said.

'When you left I thought that was it,' she said. 'What changed?'

'It turns out I actually do want to make the world a better place.' I pulled my hair back into a ponytail I was hoping made me look cute and not twelve.

'That's the spirit.' She looked down at her phone screen and said, 'There's a few here. Do you want me to ring them while you're gone?'

'Do you think they'll be there at 6pm on a Sunday afternoon?'

'Someone's got to feed the animals.'

While she did that I went in search of Rick. I checked the gym, the canteen and even the library, but he wasn't at any of them. Finally I ran into Mike, one of the other Riot Squad Boys, and he said he'd pass the message on to Rick that I was looking for him. I returned to my room hoping Susie had been more successful than I had.

She was sitting on my bed with her hands over her face.

'What's wrong?' I said. And then I smelt it. 'Holy Batman.' I pinched my nose between my thumb and first finger.

'What did you feed him?' she said through her fingers.

'Pizza.'

'Is it the cheese?'

'I think it's the salami. How did you go?'

'Nothing.'

'Really? Nothing?'

'They're all full,' she said.

'Christ, what am I going to do?' I'd been so confident with Plan A I hadn't even thought of Plan B.

'Sleep on it,' she said. 'It will all sort itself out in the morning. Just you wait and see.'

I tried really, really hard but was unable to share her blind optimism.

Chapter Four

And *That's* How We Do It Where I Came From

I'm sure if it had been Susie's dog we were hiding in the Academy it all would have worked out just peachy the next morning. But it wasn't Susie's dog. It was mine. So instead I shouldn't have been shocked when Sergeant Moores pulled a surprise room inspection. Apart from the fact I had no time to get Cocoa out, my room was a mess and my laundry undone.

I could hear him progressing his way down the hall, yelling and screaming at the other students. If I got caught with Cocoa in my room it was all over, I was sure of it.

I shoved the mess on my floor under the bed with Cocoa and placed my bag in front of him. 'Stay,' I said in a stern voice, desperately hoping he wouldn't decide to play with his squeaky pig.

'Miss Smith?'

'Yes Sergeant,' I said, jumping to my feet.

I saluted and stood to attention trying not to grimace as he ran his finger across my dusty window ledge. A week's worth of laundry tumbled over his shiny shoes when he opened the wardrobe, and my shirts hung in all their crumpled glory. The men's underpants I'd purchased to uphold the chaffing story were rumpled from my accessing the women's ones hidden underneath. My bed was unmade and my desk littered with open study books. All in all it was a pretty poor effort. I would have been worried even if I hadn't been hiding an illegal immigrant under my bed.

Sergeant Moores finished his inspection and turned to face me.

'Get it over with and go away,' I thought, watching the grim expression on his face. I was trying hard not to imagine what would happen if squeaky pig noises suddenly came from under the bed.

'Miss Smith,' he said, 'I've been doing room inspections for the last fifteen years and I can honestly say I have never seen such a ...' His voice had been increasing in volume as he whipped himself into a frenzy, but I didn't get the chance to find out what it was he had never seen before because at that moment a smell so foul, so intense that we were both forced to cover our noses, invaded the room.

I froze in horror. It looked like Cocoa's salami was the gift that kept on giving. Sergeant Moores' eyes bulged over the top of his hand and I did the only thing I could think of to waylay his suspicion.

'Excuse me,' I said.

His eyebrows rode up his forehead to his impressive head of hair as he took his hand away from his nose and opened his mouth to speak. Another wave of putrid air washed over us even worse than the last.

I put my hands to my belly and grimaced. 'Dairy intolerance,' I said. The smell kept on coming as Sergeant Moores attempted to draw breath. 'And gluten,' I added, apologetically.

He walked out to the hallway, took his hand away from his face and said, 'You need to get that looked at.' And then he left.

I closed the door before I flopped onto the bed and let out a sigh of relief. 'Come here boy,' I said softly. I could hear movement under the bed and then Cocoa commando crawled out. He trotted over to the door and whined, looking over his shoulder at me.

I was about to put him in the backpack when there was a knock at the door.

'Susie?' I said.

'It's Rick.'

I shoved Cocoa into the wardrobe before opening the door.

'Hi,' I said brightly, desperately hoping the smell had dissipated. I was guessing by the way his face screwed up that it hadn't.

'It wasn't me,' I said. I could feel my face going red.

He looked past me into the room. 'Well who was it then?'

I dragged him in to my room and shut the door. I could hear Cocoa scrabbling, frantically trying to get out of the wardrobe.

'Don't tell me,' Rick said, 'it was the ghost that lives in your wardrobe.'

I let Cocoa out before opening the window as wide as it would go.

'Is this why you were looking for me?' Rick asked.

'No. I was going to ask if you would train Susie and me in the evenings.'

'Why not,' he said, shrugging his shoulders.

'Really?'

'Got nothing better to do.'

I tried to take that as a compliment.

Cocoa wandered over and sniffed Rick's boots. His efforts were rewarded with a scratch behind the ears. He groaned and leaned into him.

'He likes you.'

'My mother had a schnauzer,' Rick said, working his fingers deep into Cocoa's beard. I pictured him kneading my flesh in the same way and tried unsuccessfully to prevent the shiver that ran over me. Why oh why hadn't I hitched up my boobs before I'd opened the door?

'What are you going to do with him?' he asked.

I sighed and then filled him in on my predicament.

'I might be able to help you out,' he said when I'd finished.

'Really?'

'I know the guy who runs the Police Dog Training School. We might be able to get him a cage there.'

'Not with a Police Dog?'

'No, they often have empty cages.'

'You have no idea how grateful I'd be,' I said, hoping he might ask for a totally inappropriate form of payment.

'Let me take him with me. If he can't I'll keep him at my room until we can find somewhere for him.'

I kissed Cocoa goodbye and put him in the back pack. 'Oh,' I said as Rick was leaving, 'he might need to go to the toilet.'

'You think?' Rick said, wrinkling up his nose.

A sense of humour as well? The guy was one in a million.

***

Rick was waiting for me outside our last class for that day – NSW Policy and Law.

'All good,' he informed me, holding up his hand for a high five.

I gladly claimed the high five, wishing I could also do a chest bump.

'Seven thirty tonight?' he asked as Susie joined us. I saw some of the other girls in our class look in our direction.

'Sounds good,' I said. I know I should have asked them if they wanted to join us, but I was loath to share him.

Susie and I checked on Cocoa at the dog kennels before we went to dinner. We walked down the aisle between the cages, clutching each other and squealing as Alsatians lunged from both sides.

A man approached us from the other end of the cages. He was holding a long shovel and I had a sudden feeling we had wandered into a horror movie. I tried to be brave, but with the barking and shaking of the fencing wire combined with a slight claustrophobia, by the time the man reached us I was ready to bolt in the opposite direction. Susie was making small squeaky noises in time with her rapid breathing so I was guessing she was feeling the same way.

He stopped a couple of metres from us and held up his hands. 'I come in peace,' he said, a huge grin on his face.

Susie and I relaxed our grip on each other and straightened up.

'Chanel?' he said.

'Hi, umm…' I realised Rick hadn't mentioned his name.

'Andy.' He held his hand out for us to shake. 'Sly dog Rick didn't tell me you were a total babe,' he said, looking me up and down.

I could feel myself blushing.

'Of course,' he said, 'being gay and everything he probably didn't notice.'

'He's gay?' I said.

'Gay as a large group of really happy people.'

'Oh.' I tried to hide my bitter disappointment by introducing Susie.

Andy winked at her, soliciting a bout of nervous giggles, and then he led us further down the aisle to the cage closest to the Dog Squad Headquarters. Cocoa was very happy to see us, jumping up and down against the wire of the cage.

'Sit,' Andy said in a deep booming voice.

Susie and I dropped to squatting positions behind him before we realised he was talking to Cocoa not us. Cocoa also stopped his jumping and sat.

'Good boy,' Andy said. He thankfully hadn't seen us sit. He opened the cage and handed Cocoa a treat, and then said, 'Down,' while he lowered his hand.

Cocoa obediently lay down and stayed there.

'Shit,' I said, as I helped Susie stand. She was giggling too hard to get up by herself. 'I tried to train him to sit, but I never succeeded.'

'You have to mean it,' Andy said, handing Cocoa another reward. 'Up,' he said, at which point Cocoa jumped up.

'Can I pat him?' I asked.

'He's your dog.'

'Not that you'd know it,' I mumbled as I pulled Cocoa into my arms. He responded enthusiastically enough to make me feel better about myself.

'I can help you train him while he's here,' Andy said. 'It would be my pleasure.' I wasn't sure if he was talking to me or to my boobs.

'What else is there for him to learn?'

Andy's laugh was earthy and honest. I decided I liked him, even if he was still staring at my chest. 'Stay, come, roll over, attack.'

I wasn't sure how I felt about the attack part, but then I thought about Mum and realised maybe a dog that attacked on command wasn't such a bad thing.

'Thanks,' I said. 'How much is it going to cost me to board him here?' I was crossing my fingers and hoping it wasn't going to be too expensive. Hairdressing hadn't paid well, and most of my wage had gone on clothes. Now I was without an income and pretty much all of my savings had gone to fund my police training.

'Well seeing as how we don't officially board animals, perhaps a carton of beer would do it,' he said.

A carton of beer? That I could afford.

After we had made a time for me to learn how to train Cocoa, Susie and I headed back to the mess. I was helping myself to a slab of potato bake oozing with white sauce and cheese when Rick appeared by my side with two plates, each containing a portion of steamed fish and some vegetables.

'What's this?' I said in dismay as he handed them to Susie and me.

'If you want me to train you, you have to eat what I tell you to eat.'

'But there won't be enough energy in this to get me through another work out,' Susie whimpered. Her plate had been piled high with roast chicken, potato bake and roast pumpkin. 'I need some carbohydrates.'

'This is carbohydrates,' Rick said, gesturing at the broccoli. 'Besides,' he continued, looking at me with a grin on his face, 'Sergeant Moores has advised the cooks of your dairy and gluten intolerances.'

I pulled a face at him as I contemplated the ramifications. No more ice-cream? No more custard? No more cake? Oh well, there was always the jelly.

We ate our nutritious dinner and then headed over to the gym. I was feeling a little nervous at the thought of the training session. It hadn't been so bad when Susie and I had been training ourselves. We had warmed up on the running machine – at a pace that allowed us to talk, and then randomly moved around the weight equipment.

It was better and worse than I thought it would be. Better because he tailored a weight program for each of us to follow, worse because he mentioned a guy named Sam a few times and it became obvious that Andy was right. He was gay. Perving at him just didn't give me the same satisfaction any more.

The weeks flitted by with our new routine. Between lessons, study, dog training and physical training I didn't even have time to go clothes shopping, which was good as I couldn't afford it. Plus, we had started weapons training, which took up a serious chunk of my concentration as I tried to shoot the target, and not one of the other students.

I wasn't sure why, but Sergeant Moores had backed right off since the farting incident. I waited in fear for Nastacia to get me back for my accidental spying but as the weeks went by and she didn't I started to relax. I caught her watching me a few times, a strange expression on her face but she never confronted me. In the end I surmised they had gotten bored with tormenting me. I didn't care why; I was just relieved things had taken a turn for the better.

Susie's clothes started to hang off her, and even mine were a little loose. We were measured up for our new uniforms, and even though the shoes were a disaster, I was proud to wear mine around campus. It meant we were almost there, almost policewomen. I couldn't wait to see the look on my Mum's face at our graduation ceremony.

She had been released from hospital but Andy said it was fine for Cocoa to stay there - I think he had a soft spot for him, and I was enjoying having him near me. Although I almost had heart failure when I went to visit him and found him joining in on the police dog training.

They were teaching the dogs to attack, and the trainers had padding on their forearms which they fed into the dogs' mouths on the command. The padding was black and furry and I had an awful feeling one of the other dogs would mistake Cocoa for it and tear him apart.

'Attack,' Andy yelled. Cocoa charged towards him and leapt, fastening onto Andy's padded arm. He growled ferociously as Andy shook his arm from side to side. The fact that his tail was waving madly the whole time only made him slightly less scary.

As soon as Andy called release Cocoa let go and trotted back to the start line. He touched noses with one of the Alsatians, a feat which had my heart in my throat, and then sat; his entire focus on Andy. I couldn't help but notice how his walk had changed. He used to bounce like a puppy now he strutted, his head held high. And just like that I realised my little boy had grown up. It was a bitter sweet moment.

***

'Relax, breathe,' I said to Susie. We were in the mess hall waiting for our physical exam to start and Susie was slipping ever closer to hysterics. 'Rick said you're fit enough to pass.'

It was true. With Rick's forced diet (you are what you eat) and his strict exercise regime, Susie had transformed over the last five months. She still had the helium balloon voice, but she no longer resembled one. I wouldn't have recognised her if I hadn't seen it happen.

We had sat the weapons exam the day before. I had aced the theory but only narrowly scraped through the practical. (It turns out that aiming at the target is far easier than actually hitting it.) While confident with the theory exams from that morning even I was a little nervous about the physical exam. No-one – not even Rick – would tell us everything it entailed.

'You have to eat something.'

'I think I'm going to vomit,' she said weakly.

'If you don't eat something you probably will vomit,' I said.

The beginning of the exam was the part we had been expecting: sit-ups, push-ups, and a strength test. Then there was the beep test – where beep is not a replacement for a swear word but is instead the timed beep a machine makes as you sprint back and forth between two lines. The beeps get closer together making you sprint faster and faster until you're well and truly beeped.

It had always been Susie's weakness so I breathed a sigh of relief when she made it to the minimum requirement time for passing.

'I wonder what the last part is,' I said to her. The only thing Rick would tell us was that there was a surprise at the end of the exam.

We watched as Rick approached a white line painted on the grass. He had a box in one hand and a stopwatch in the other. 'Right,' he said, gesturing for us all to gather around. For the last part you'll be doing the five kilometre obstacle course. But,' he added, 'it will be timed.'

They always were so that was no surprise.

'And,' he added with an evil grin, 'you'll be doing it handcuffed to a partner.'

That put a bit of a spin on things, but it still wasn't too bad. I was sure Susie and I could handle it.

'And,' he continued, 'I will be choosing the pairs.'

We waited while he pulled our names out of the box and paired us up. Susie was cuffed to Liam, the tallest boy on our course. She looked ridiculous with her hand hanging suspended at chest height.

My name was the second last one to be pulled out of the box. Rick tipped the last piece of paper out, took a look at the name and then shot me a cute grin. Geez I still couldn't believe he was gay. When he didn't read the other name out immediately I glanced around, looking for the only other free person in our course, and immediately all thoughts of how spunky Rick was were driven from my mind. *Oh dear Lord no.*

'Nastaaaciaaa.' It must have been the buzzing in my ears that made it sound like he called her name out in slow motion. Surely he wouldn't be that cruel. The only consolation, and it was a small one, was that the look on her face was what I imagined was on mine – total horror.

We stood as far from each other as was possible as he handcuffed us. Even then it was too close. We hadn't had any contact since the day I saw her girlfriend and I had really liked it that way.

Rick sent us off with two minutes between each set of couples. Liam and Susie were before us and the two minutes between felt like a lifetime, partly because I was nervous and partly because it was awkward as hell being handcuffed to Nastacia. My nerves made me want to crack lame jokes, but somehow I didn't think she would find my pink fluffy handcuff quips amusing.

We had done this course numerous times during our training, but from the first obstacle it became apparent that it had all changed. It used to start with a log climb, now there was a long tunnel of netting. Commando crawling is hard enough when you're not handcuffed to someone, when you are it requires a huge amount of coordination. Unfortunately Nastacia and I were employing zero teamwork in our bid to pretend this wasn't happening.

We got half way through the tunnel, yanking and tugging at each other's arm, before she got far enough ahead of me to whip my hand up towards my face. My fist was clenched and it made a sickening crunchy sound as it connected with my nose.

'Yeeoww,' I screeched. Even though it was *my* fist, I didn't see it coming. I stared cross eyed at my nose trying to determine if there was any damage.

Nastacia stared back over her shoulder at me, an exasperated look on her face.

'Am I bleeding?' I said.

'No, you're still perfect.' Her voice was snippy.

'This obviously isn't working,' I said.

She looked like she wanted to disagree purely for the sake of it but there was nothing to disagree about. 'We need to crawl opposite each other.'

'No we need to go in the same direction,' I said.

She huffed. 'Of course we need to go in the same direction.' She shook her arm attached to me as she said it. 'You need to crawl with your left leg up while I have my right up.'

'Oh. Like walking and holding hands.'

'Trust you to think of that.'

'What the hell is that supposed to mean?'

Rather than answer me, she started crawling. It was a toss-up between making a stand and punching myself in the nose again or continuing. I'd like to think it was the diplomat in me that decided to go on, but I suspect it was the cowardly lion.

I managed to stay in opposite time with her and the rest of the tunnel progressed smoothly. We emerged and navigated the next few obstacles while stoically ignoring each other, which, given our circumstances, was quite a feat. That all changed when we got to the mud pit.

'I do not want to fall in that,' I said, as I grasped one side of the flying fox t-bar which would carry us over the pit.

'Wouldn't want to ruin your hair.' Nastacia pivoted to face me and grabbed the other side of the bar. Her body pushed up against mine feeling awkwardly intimate.

'You know there's more to me than how I look,' I said.

She raised an eyebrow and said, 'Most people don't classify mindless bimboism as a talent.'

'You … total … bitch,' I said from between clenched teeth. A red haze started to obscure my vision of her smug expression.

'Oh look, it has teeth.'

I felt her body tense but in the heat of the moment forgot we were hanging from a flying fox. She pushed us off the edge as I was saying, 'I don't know what I ever did to make you hate meeeaaahhhhhhh.' We whistled through the air and landed in a tumble of limbs on the other side of the mud.

'You were born,' she hissed, climbing off me.

I've always been a bit of a pacifist, make love not war and all that, but she had pushed my buttons for months and now I didn't know why I had let her. All of a sudden I wanted to teach her a lesson for bullying me. I wanted revenge and I wanted it badly.

I kicked a leg out, sweeping her feet from under her, and as she landed on her back I jumped on top of her. I'd never been in a fight before and I realise now the ones I'd seen in movies were all perfectly choreographed. So it came as a bit of a surprise to me how awkward and ineffective a fight can be. *Especially* when you're handcuffed to the person you're fighting.

I used my free arm to pull her hair as she slapped at me. Then she shifted her weight and rolled over, forcing us onto our knees where we shoved and pulled while shrieking and squealing. The force of our movements opposing each other caused our handcuffed arms to swing around like a crazy pendulum.

'Take it back,' I yelled as we clambered to our feet.

'No.'

'Take it back or else.'

'Or what, you'll tell Mummy on me?'

I let out a bellow of rage and threw myself at her in my best impression of a football tackle. I felt my shoulder connect with her stomach, heard the woof of air express from her lungs and had a second to feel pleased with my efforts before we were flying backwards, airborne again as we flew out over and then down into the pool of mud.

I landed on top of her with a mushy splat, pressing her into the gooey mess. It was perfect. Putting a hand on her face I shoved till the mud seeped over the top of her cheeks. She roared and locked out her free arm, wrapping her hand around my throat. It hurt, but with only one arm it was a pretty ineffective choke hold. I slapped my forearm into the inner part of her elbow, breaking her hold on my neck, and pushed her arm down under my knee where I pinned it with my weight. Then I grabbed a handful of mud.

'Guess you don't do girlie stuff like mud packs,' I said as I dribbled the muck onto her face. I took great delight in smearing it all over her head as she shook it from side to side. 'Oh no,' I said, tssking at her. 'Look what you made me do. You made me goop.'

She screeched and shoved her handcuffed arm out to the side. The manoeuvre took me by surprise and threw me off her before I could compensate by shifting my weight. I managed to land on my knees but she jumped on my back and started forcing my head down towards the mud. I braced my body and resisted but she had her whole bodyweight on me and painstakingly slowly the mud got closer and closer.

'This is how we do a mud pack where I come from,' she snarled.

I took a deep breath and closed my eyes just before my face entered the mud. The cool sludge flowed over my skin and in a different circumstance it probably would have felt quite nice. But it wasn't a different circumstance, it was a fight. As things stood I was losing, and if I didn't do something in the next thirty seconds I was going to lose more than just the fight. Panic bubbled to the surface with my overwhelming fear of drowning and in pure desperation I let an elbow drop, throwing my weight to the side and her off my back.

I took a deep breath of air, wiped the mud away from my eyes and said, 'Oh and exactly where do you come from? Hell?'

The weight on my arm slackened and she made a gurgling noise. I opened my eyes slightly, blinking rapidly to dispel any mud, and looked at her. She was slumped in the mud, laughing so hard that tears were making clear little rivers through the mud on her face.

'You look awful,' she managed to choke out, pointing at my face.

I looked at her in amazement, so shocked by her laughter that I forgot to be angry, and then I started to laugh as well. We were totally covered in mud. There wasn't a square centimetre which hadn't been coated.

'You look like a giant dog turd,' I said, throwing more mud at her.

'You look like a ginormous cow pat.' She hurled a wad back and it smacked into my chest.

'Oh no.' I brushed ineffectively at the lump. 'You got mud on my shirt.'

She laughed again as she clambered to her feet pulling me up with her. 'Look at the state of us.'

'What is Rick going to think?' I said as we started to run again.

'I didn't think you'd mind Rick seeing you all dirty.'

I snorted. 'He's gay.'

'Rick?'

'Yeah. Total shame.'

'No he's not.'

'Andy, the head of the Police Dog Squad, told me. And he should know because he's his friend.'

'Andy's a shit stirrer,' she said as we climbed over a pile of wood.

'But he talks about his boyfriend Sam all the time.'

She started laughing, and we had to slow down so she could run and laugh at the same time.

'What's so funny,' I finally demanded.

'Sam is short for Samantha,' she said between giggles.

Well I'll be damned, so he wasn't gay.

'I wish I had known you thought he was gay,' she said.

'Why?'

'I would have gotten a kick out of it.'

The silence caused by the animosity behind her words hung over us like a heavy fog as we ran to the balance log.

We were half way across, her going backwards, when I finally summoned the guts to ask the question. 'Why would you have gotten a kick out of it?'

She glanced down into my eyes and said, 'I'm not sure.' We wavered on the log for a few seconds before she broke eye contact and started moving backwards again.

The silence between us was different now as we dodged and weaved through the course. Initially it had been cold and distant. A silence born of two people ignoring each other, but we couldn't do that anymore. Something had broken, and not in a bad way, and now the silence was loaded with tension.

We were traversing the zigzag ropes when she said, 'I'm sorry.'

I was so shocked I hooked my foot on a rope and would have fallen if not for her support. 'Sorry for the leaky pen?'

'Yes.'

'The men's underwear?'

'Especially sorry about that.'

'The spiders?'

'The what?'

'The huge hairy spiders you put in my room.'

She shuddered. 'I didn't put any spiders in your room.'

Huh. Maybe they did travel in packs.

We ran up a hill and could see the last obstacle looming in the distance. 'Oh no,' I said.

'A rock climbing wall,' Nastacia confirmed.

I could see Susie and her partner part way up the wall. As we watched Susie slipped, dragging Liam off with her. Poor Susie, even without the handcuffs she would have had trouble climbing it. I could see Liam gesturing and then she pulled herself up onto his chest and wrapped her legs around him. She clung on like a back-to-front, one-armed koala while he clambered awkwardly up to the top and then disappeared from view.

'We are so not doing it like that,' Nastacia said.

'Afraid I'd drop you?'

She snorted. 'I know you'd drop me.'

We fell off the wall twice before we made it to the top; partly because our hands were slippery from the mud and partly because we had trouble finding handgrips big enough for us both to hang onto. Coming down was as scary as going up and we slipped with a metre to go, tumbling to the earth.

'I hope we don't lose points for the dismount,' I said.

'Why didn't you tell?' Nastacia asked, her gaze drilling into me.

'Tell what?'

'On me. That day.'

'Ooohh. *That* day.' I pulled her arm in the direction we had to go and started running again. The finish line was only a few hundred metres away. 'Why would I?'

'You could have had me kicked out of the Academy.'

'They said we couldn't have people of the opposite sex in our room,' I pointed out.

'It didn't even cross your mind did it?'

'No.'

We ran for a little longer before she said, 'That really sucks.'

'What does?' The finish line came into view in the distance and we quickened our pace.

'All this time I've hated you because I thought you weren't good enough, and now it turns out you may be a better person than me.'

'What's this 'may be' shit?' I asked as we charged across the finish line.

'All right so there's every possibility you are a better person.'

We slowed to a walk and then stopped.

'That didn't hurt did it?' I said, grinning up at her. And then I had a thought. 'Is that why you backed off? Because you thought I was going to dob?'

'Yes. And then when you didn't I asked Uncle Miles to leave you alone.'

'Uncle Miles?'

'Also known as Sergeant Moores.'

I glared at her.

She shrugged. 'I told you I come from a family of policemen.'

'What the hell were you two doing?' Rick asked in dismay as he looked us up and down.

We held our wrists out for him to undo the cuffs. 'Mud wrestling,' I said, giving him my cutest smile. I was sure the effect was totally ruined by the clumps of dried mud that were starting to flake off, but I didn't care. I had a lot of lost flirting time to make up for.

Susie came running over and threw her arms around me. 'We did it,' she squealed, immediately letting go again. 'Urghh you're disgusting.'

'Oh my God we've finished.' My astounding conversation with Nastacia had driven the importance of the obstacle course from my mind.

'Liam's invited us into town to celebrate.' Susie blushed when she said it. I glanced over at him and saw him staring at Susie, a goofy look on his face. 'Do you want to go?'

'Of course,' I said. Who was I to get in the way of young love?' 'Want to come?' I said to Nastacia.

I'm not sure if Susie or Nastacia was more surprised at my invitation, but I could tell Susie was so happy to be going where Liam was that she probably wouldn't have minded if I'd told her we had to dance with the devil.

'You're inviting me after everything I did to you?' Nastacia said.

'I don't hold grudges.'

'I'll need time to shower.'

I laughed. 'And I was going to go like this?'

'Can I bring my girlfriend?'

'Love to meet her.'

'It's official,' she sighed sadly, 'you are a better person than me.'

Chapter Five

You Always Remember Your First

'Home sweet home,' I said, checking to make sure that the number on the building matched the one on the piece of paper I was holding. It did. I wasn't happy about it. Everything about this building screamed, 'Suspicious death'. Of course I may have been overreacting to the ominous feeling exuding from the dank mouldy brickwork. I hoped it was that and not a new psychic ability I'd developed overnight.

Cocoa stirred in the backpack trying to get comfortable and I hurried up the stairs as fast as I could while dragging my huge suitcase. It wouldn't do to have anybody asking me questions about my possessed bag. Animals were strictly forbidden and I had lied out of desperation to secure the short term rental.

The outside of the building hadn't quite prepared me for the flat. Tiny and dark, the walls were stained with water marks and the air thick with a damp stench. Paint flaked and peeled from the ceiling and the carpet was thread worn to the point of being non-existent in places.

'Pretty,' I muttered, staring at the holey orange and brown swirl curtains. Oh well, at least it had curtains. The wardrobe was a total disaster, clearly designed for people who believed that one set of clothing was enough. And the bathroom – well the bathroom looked like the recently deserted site of a mould warfare experiment. But there was a lock on the front door and a bed, so for now it was home.

Cocoa didn't seem too disturbed by the ugly carpet as he snuffled around the room. I put his bed near mine and he jumped into it, turning around a few times to rough it up before settling down.

Tomorrow was my first day 'on the beat', and I was trying to ignore the butterflies currently using my stomach as a Grand Prix track. The postings had come out a couple of weeks ago telling me to get my butt to King's Cross. (Not in those actual words of course.) I'd never been to Sydney before let alone the famous King's Cross. But I'd heard there were some top designer studios located in the district and even though most of my shopping would be done through windows, it was better than nothing.

Susie was staying in Goulburn near her family and our parting had been a sad one. I wasn't sure I would have made it through those earlier days at the Academy without her. But then again, she didn't think she would have made it through to the end without me, so I guessed we were even.

Noise from the street below rumbled up through my window; a jumble of music and people talking and cars honking, making it impossible to get to sleep for any period of time. I woke groggy and disgruntled, promising myself, as I staggered into the bathroom, that I would find a new apartment as soon as possible. I closed my eyes as the hot water of the shower streamed over my body, partly to sneak in an extra few minutes sleep but mostly to block out the sight of the mouldy walls. 'Tonight,' I said to the tiny cubicle, 'you, me and a bottle of bleach.'

The shower and the strong cups of coffee I consumed before leaving for work helped get my head back in the game, but they didn't help with those damned butterflies.

'How do I look?' I asked Cocoa. I was feeling like a bit of a phoney in my uniform. He glanced up from his grooming and tilted his head to one side before resuming where he had left off.

'Yeah you're right, I need to look taller.' I pulled my hairstyle out and redid the bun, positioning it near the top of my head. Then I spent several moments admiring the caramel highlights I had finally gotten around to doing.

When I could stall no longer I grabbed my stuff and walked up the road to my new place of work. The police station was smaller than I'd expected. An unobtrusive building, except for the police cars parked out the front. A herd of elephants joined the butterflies in my stomach and for a moment I was worried I might be sick.

I descended the stairs from the street level to the front door and entered. The foyer was bare except for a variety of plastic seats lining the wall, and a nearly dead pot plant in the corner. Someone had left a few tattered magazines lying on one of the chairs.

The wall to the left of the entry had a large cut out area which housed the reception desk and a small office. A small sticker on the desk said, 'Beware, panic screen installed.' A friendly looking man in uniform stood behind the desk watching me.

'Hi,' I said, showing him my badge.

'You must be Chanel.'

I noted the three stripes on his shoulder. 'Yes Sergeant...'

'Walker,' he said. 'But you can call me Dave. I'm the Sergeant in charge of the team you've been assigned to so we'll have plenty of time to get to know each other. For now though Inspector Ramy is waiting to debrief you.' He pulled a funny face as he said it and then pointed me down the hall to another office.

I knocked nervously on the door and entered on instructions of the gruff, 'Come in'. I was surprised to see Daniel, one of the other students from my course, already standing in front of the desk. Tall and skinny with dark blonde hair, Daniel was painfully shy. His bottle end glasses only added to his awkwardness by making his eyes appear twice as large as they were. I hadn't had much to do with him on course and hadn't realised he had been posted here as well.

'Ahh Chanel,' the man I was assuming was Inspector Ramy said, 'just in time to avoid being late.' I wasn't sure if I was being chastised or not. 'You'll find your desks in the muster room with operational manuals on them. I want you to spend the next few days reading through them and familiarising yourself with how things are done in this station.'

He looked back at his desk and started leafing through paperwork. We were still standing there when he looked back up a few moments later. 'Well, what are you waiting for?' he said.

'For you to dismiss us,' I felt like saying. But I didn't. The last thing I needed was to get on his bad side on my first day. I was sure it would happen eventually. It seemed to be the pattern of my life, through no apparent fault of my own (or none that I could determine), I ended up on the wrong side of authority figures.

Daniel and I filed out of the room and looked around the hall. 'Left or right?' I said.

'Left,' Daniel replied.

I wasn't sure if he knew or if it was a good guess but we turned left and sure enough found a large room filled with desks and phones. There were three other police already in the room; one was making coffee while the other two were pulling donuts out of a large box. I got a couple of things out of that. The first was that that there was a Krispy Kreme donut shop nearby and the second was that I was going to have to find a gym.

The man making the coffee looked up when we walked in. 'You,' he said pointing at me, 'Heads or tails?'

'Pardon?'

'Heads or tails?'

'Heads,' I said.

'Congrats. You're the new coffee girl.' He put the cups down and walked over to the donut box. I had a feeling that even if I had said tails I would have lost.

'Hi yourself,' I said. There were two empty desks with large manuals sitting on them. The one located conveniently near the urn and fridge had my name badge sitting on it which bore out my suspicion about the heads and tails game being fixed. Daniel's desk was on the other side of the room. Typical.

'Let me guess,' I said, looking at the man, 'it was a two tailed coin.'

He chuckled sheepishly.

'Fine,' I said, taking up the cup, 'but there better be some donuts for me.'

After I had learnt their names - Bob, Nathan and Mark - and made their coffee, nobly resisting the urge to spit in it, I sat down with my donut and started to leaf through the operations manual. It was thick, and I'm talking doorstopper thick. The sort of thing that was guaranteed to put me into a temporary coma.

'Old Ramy's got you reading that has he?' Bob said. He was positioned at the desk closest to me.

I nodded my head. 'I'm thinking I can carry it around with me as a weapon.'

'What about your Glock?'

'My clock?'

'Your gun. Haven't you been issued with it yet?'

'No.' I mean I knew we were going to have weapons, and we had done the appropriate training on course, but now that the moment was finally here I was more than a little scared. What if I shot someone? I mean I know there was a chance throughout my career that I would be forced to shoot someone in the line of fire. But what if I shot the wrong person? Or more embarrassing, what if I shot myself? If I didn't kill myself I'd be laughed off the Force.

'Right, well, we better get that sorted,' Bob said.

Daniel hadn't been fitted out either, so Bob put himself in charge of us for the morning and drove us into town where the weapons and uniforms were held.

'Have you started the first assignment yet?' Daniel asked me during the drive.

'Sure,' I lied. In truth I had been putting off the moment I started the one year of study I still needed to complete before I could lose the probationary part of my title, Probationary Constable. Never having fully read the course information it had come as quite a shock to me after graduation.

Two hours later I was the proud owner of a Glock 22. I also had handcuffs (I was looking forward to using them), capsicum spray, an expandable baton, a portable radio and a first aid kit.

'Where on earth do we keep all this stuff?' I said.

'Here,' Bob handed me a belt and then looked me up and down. 'On second thoughts,' he said, taking the belt back. He returned a few minutes later with a vest. 'The circumference of your waist is too small to house everything.' He pointed at his own expansive girth where his belt easily held all of the required items. 'This will work better for you and you'll be more comfortable.'

'Thanks.' I spent the next hour back at the station arranging my vest, working out the best way to house the assortment of goodies I'd received in its pockets. Unfortunately after that it was back to the drudgery of reading the manual. I amused myself by playing with my expandable baton in an attempt to stay awake.

'I like a girl who knows how to handle a baton.'

I looked up from my manual, unsuccessfully trying to close my mouth while I gawked at the speaker. His face was a heavenly mixture of cheekbones, eyelashes and kissable lips. His nose had been broken in the past but the asymmetry managed to add to his looks by injecting a dash of bad boy to his blonde haired, angelic profile. Add to all this a body that, even through the confines of his suit, you could tell spent hours in the gym and an English accent and I had to grip the edge of the table to stop myself jumping it to dry hump his leg.

I wanted to say something witty in reply, but I had been staring at him with my mouth hanging open and if I didn't say something soon he was going to think I was simple.

'Hello,' I said. *Great*, now he was definitely going to think I was simple.

He came over to perch on the corner of my desk, so close I could smell his aftershave. *Good God*. Was it possible that he could be even more handsome close up?

'I also like a good bun,' he said, peering down at my hair. His eyes were a startling shade of blue. I found myself staring straight into them, holding my breath.

'Detective Senior Sergeant Roger Richardson at your service,' he said holding out his hand. His accent was totally dreamy.

I took it in mine and, still gazing into his eyes, said, 'Probationary Constable Chanel Bun. Oh... I mean Smith.'

Christ. Did I really just say that?

'Constable Bun,' he said, smiling, 'it's a pleasure to meet you.'

I gave him my cutest smile, hoping I didn't have any donut stuck on my front teeth, and wishing I could think of something intelligent to say.

'What do you say to coming for a ride with me?'

I desperately wanted to go, but I didn't want to get into trouble on my first day. 'I'm meant to be reading the manual,' I said, hoping that didn't make me sound like a loser.

'Let me have a word with Ramy,' he said, gliding off my desk.

I watched him walk across the room towards the hall, trying to think what his walk reminded me of. It wasn't till he was on his way back a few minutes later that I got it. He moved like a lion, or a tiger. Like a predator.

'Come on Constable Bun,' he said, 'we're out of here.'

It was ridiculous how much pleasure I got out of his use of the word 'we'. I was going to have to get a grip or make a total dick of myself.

'Got your gun?' he said.

'Ahuh.' The weight of the vest with the gun, baton, torch and spray was going to take some getting used to.

'Is there one in the barrel?'

'Pardon?'

'Have they showed you where to load it?'

I shook my head, a bit embarrassed that I had been about to embark on my first foray as a policewoman with an unloaded gun.

'Come on,' he said. He took me down to the gun locker. 'We can only go in one at a time so I'll have to tell you what to do. In there you'll find a gun loading machine. You always load your gun with it facing into the machine.'

'In case I misfire?'

'Exactly.'

I opened the door to the locker room.

'Oh,' he said, 'you'll find your locker in there with a padlock on it. That's where your gun lives when you're not working.'

I nodded my head. 'Anything else?'

'Just smile for the cameras.'

I entered the locker room and looked around. Cameras were located in the four corners of the room filming the two rows of lockers that ran back to back down the centre. I could see one with my name on it. A padlock with a key sticking out of it hung from the latch.

At the far end was the gun-loading machine. I put my hand in there with the gun, barrel facing away from me, and inserted the magazine. Then I pulled back on the top, chambering a round.

I was insanely nervous about holding the loaded weapon. I mean I know I'd done it before but this was different. There was no-one here to tell me if what I was doing was right. I carefully placed the loaded gun in the holster and went back out to where Roger was waiting.

'So what are we doing?' I asked, trying to make my voice sound nonchalant. I didn't do a very good job and instead it was tinged with excitement.

Roger flashed a grin at me. 'We're going to drive around and play my favourite game.'

I was dying to know what his favourite game was. Was it at all possible that it was catch and kiss?

'We're going to play let's imagine who's breaking the law.'

Oh. *That* game.

We drove around for about an hour, taking turns to point out people and guess what they were up to. A man on his cell phone was suddenly a drug dealer calling in an order. A woman walking up the street in a short skirt was a lady of the night on an early shift. A girl fighting with a man was a victim of domestic abuse.

I hadn't had so much fun in ages.

We worked our way down to the other end of King's Cross – the seedy part, as Roger called it – and were heading back to the station when Roger said, 'That's weird.'

'What's weird?'

He pulled the car over next to the curb in a no standing zone (ahhh, the perks of being a policeman) and stopped.

'The lane back there. There are normally some hookers hanging out near the entry.'

'Even during the day?'

'No rest for the wicked.'

'Maybe they've gone for coffee.'

'No. They guard their territory pretty well. They would have left at least one here.' He hopped out of the car and I followed suit. 'Check your weapon,' he said.

I nodded nervously and felt for it at my waist. Check – one weapon.

The lane was narrow with a long line of properties backing onto it on either side. I followed him into it, looking around nervously for would-be muggers or drug dealers.

'This was originally built as a dunny lane,' Roger said in a low voice.

'A dunny lane?' I noticed he had drawn his gun and copied him.

'Back in the day before sewerage systems, the waste was taken away up these lanes.'

It felt like a sewerage lane – oppressive and mucky, and scary to boot. My anxiety was increasing exponentially with the distance from the car; my heart beat wild, my breathing ragged. I wanted to ask him to return to the vehicle, but I couldn't. Firstly because I didn't want him to know I was scared and secondly because this was my job.

Eventually we could see the end in the distance and I felt Roger relax. 'Stupid imagination,' he said, starting to turn towards the car. But then he stopped and stiffened, staring towards the back corner of the lane.

A piece of pink chiffon fluttered in the breeze.

'Not again,' I heard Roger say, his voice a low moan of distress.

I followed him to the chiffon, my eyes travelling slowly down the bright slash of pink. My thinking was robotic as I documented that the material belonged to a blouse with pearl buttons and a sash waist and that the colour looked good against the soft crème of the short skirt. My eyes moved on, against my wishes, to a swan neck, a delicate angular cheek, before settling, finally, on the horror of her staring eyes.

She would have been pretty if she weren't covered in blood. Even through the smudge of red on her face I could see the cheekbones, the curve of her lips. Her limbs lay in a jumble, her clothes askew. It looked as if she had been fighting: her fingers curled into claws, her legs bent for kicking. Fighting until the life had left her, leaking out through the wound at her throat.

I staggered away and threw up, heaving up my donuts as tears tracked freely down my face. The image of her body was burnt into my mind; even with my eyes closed I could see her clearly.

When I was finished with the puking, I wiped my mouth on a tissue and turned back towards the woman.

'First dead body?' Roger asked.

'No, I see them all the time.'

He smiled wryly at me. 'Sorry.'

'All part of the job,' I said, shrugging. I looked away from her. All of a sudden I wasn't so sure I had finished being sick.

'Why don't you sit over there,' he said, 'while I call in backup.'

In the end I went back up the lane to wait for the rest of the crime squad. I wanted to watch them work, but I was loath to embarrass myself again, so

I got a lift back to the station with one of the other detectives.

Daniel was still diligently reading his operational manual when I arrived. I quietly took a seat at my desk and flipped the book back open.

'They found another body?' Bob, Nathan and Mark clustered around my desk.

'Ahuh.' I saw Daniel look up from his book and push his glasses up his nose.

'What do you mean *another* body?' he asked.

'Is that the fourth or the fifth?' Bob said to the others.

'The fifth,' Mark confirmed.

'Were they all prostitutes?' I asked. Roger had been sure she was one of the women who normally worked the area.

'Yep.'

'And they're always killed the same way?'

'Throat cut?' Bob asked.

'Yes.' I shuddered at the memory. I had never realised how much blood was in the human body.

'That's our serial killer.' Bob shook his head and went back to his desk.

'It gets easier with time,' Nathan said, putting a hand on my shoulder.

'I hope so,' I said, but privately I thought it would be a sadder world when I was not affected by the sight of a dead body.

***

I didn't sleep well that night. Every time I managed to fall asleep the dead woman's memory haunted me, asking me to help her. Of course, then I would wake straight up and the noise from the street would delay my return to slumber.

Daniel and I were still plugging our way through the manual the next day when Roger sauntered into work. Bob and Nathan, who were filling out some paperwork, gathered around his desk, asking him questions about the latest murder.

More for the want to do something, anything, rather than read that stupid manual, I hopped up, stretched and proceeded to make the coffee. Besides, it would give me an excuse to get closer to Roger without it looking obvious.

'Just the same as the others,' I heard him say. 'Whoever the killer is…they're good.' His voice held a note of frustration.

'So nothing for forensics?'

'No skin under her nails, or hair. It will take a bit more time to get the results for saliva and semen.'

'Nothing dropped at the scene?' I asked.

Roger looked at me standing behind the others. 'Hello Constable Bun,' he said.

I blushed and handed him a coffee. 'Milk and sugar?' I asked.

'I like 'em white and sweet.'

I blushed even harder and scuttled back to the manual. Daniel was still sitting at his desk, but he was watching Roger and the others.

'No,' Roger said, answering my question, 'nothing dropped at the scene.'

I buried my head in my book and pretended to be busy, but I was listening really hard; listening for details of the serial killer but also listening for any mention of a girlfriend, or worse yet, a wife.

They joked around for a while but there was no more talk of the serial killer. He drank his coffee, left his dirty cup on the edge of the sink, and then approached Daniel.

'Coming?' he said.

Daniel looked up through his glasses, goggling at Roger. 'Yes sir,' he said, standing up quickly.

'Detective,' Roger corrected him.

I tried to suppress my disappointment that he had taken Daniel and not me. I told myself it was only fair, seeing as how I had gotten to ride with him yesterday, but I was bored and – who am I kidding – already had a huge crush on Roger. I washed up his cup and then the rest of the day passed slowly until I got to pack up my things and go home.

Chapter Six

Why Does This Sort Of Stuff Always Happen To Me?

I bought a paper on the way home and searched the 'For Rent' pages while I ate my dinner. Then I smuggled Cocoa outside in my back pack and we went for a walk.

Sydney in October has a tangible energy; a city waking up after a long, cold winter. It was contagious and I found myself smiling as I walked.

I took Cocoa down to the dog park and released him from the lead. He ran off, nose to the ground as he sought the best place to lay his golden egg. When he had finished, I picked it up in a bag, promising myself I was going to put him on a healthier diet, and threw it into a bin. Then I sat down on a park bench that provided a view out over the city below.

I had only been there for a minute when I heard a voice say, 'Oooh, will you look at that. It's love at first sight.'

A short man, wearing tight jeans and an even tighter black t-shirt which emphasised a sculpted chest, crossed the walkway and sat down next to me.

He gestured with a hand to where Cocoa was running around with a black poodle.

'Oh,' I said. 'It's nice to see him playing with a dog his own size.' I still hadn't gotten over the sight of him playing with the Alsatians.

'I'm Bwuce,' he said.

'Bwuce?'

'No... Bewuce.'

'Oh Bruce,' I said. 'I'm Chanel.'

'That's Lancelot,' he said, pointing towards the poodle.

'Cocoa,' I said.

He let out a high pitch giggle and fluttered his hands around. 'Cocoa and Chanel, that's a good one.'

I smiled. 'Actually my ex-boyfriend named him.'

'Ooh well, he had a sense of humour. Is he still single?'

I started to laugh and then realised he was serious. 'Yes, but he doesn't live in Sydney.'

Bruce sighed. 'Shame, it's hard to find a man with a good sense of humour.'

Lancelot and Cocoa ran past us, rubbing up against each other and gently biting each other's muzzles.

'If only it were that easy,' Bruce said.

'So, there aren't a lot of gay men in King's Cross?'

'Oh nooo,' he said, 'there's heaps of them, just not a lot looking for a relationship.'

I mulled his words over and then sighed. 'I know how you feel,' I said. All of the men I had met in the last few years who had been interested in more than a roll in the hay had been dull. Thinking I was being fussy (okay, giving into Mum's nagging that I was being fussy) I had given it a shot with Tommy. The only good thing that had come out of *that* had been Cocoa.

'Why aren't the bad boys interested in relationships?' I said to Bruce.

'Girlfriend,' he said, waving his hands around, 'if they were interested in a relationship then they wouldn't be bad boys.'

I left Bruce there with a promise to meet him and Lancelot the next night, and wandered back to the apartment. It was starting to get dark and a woman in a short skirt had taken up residence on one of the street corners. Was she a prostitute? I couldn't be sure. But I was dying to ask her if she knew anything about the woman's body we had found yesterday.

I grasped my courage with both hands and walked towards her.

'Sorry sister,' she said, 'I ain't interested in that kind of action.'

Well, that answered *that* question.

'Oh no,' I said, 'neither am I. I wanted to ask you about...' I stopped, not sure how to frame the question.

'About what?' Suspicion coated her words.

'The woman whose body was found yesterday.'

She stared at me for a few seconds before asking, 'You a cop?'

'Yes,' I said.

'I don't talk to no cops,' she said, turning her back on me.

'Oh no, I'm not like that,' I said, smiling.

She continued to ignore me.

'I just want to help.' Even to my ears it sounded lame.

'You want to help?' she said, swivelling her head to look at me again.

'Yes.' I nodded my head eagerly hoping to impress her with my sincerity.

'Then go away pig. You're scaring off my customers.'

If she had slapped me it would have stunned me less. Pig? I mean I was a cop but I wasn't like ... *Like what?* I asked myself. Like all the other cops?

I sighed and headed back towards the apartment. Of course I was like all the other cops. It didn't matter that I wanted to be liked by everybody (not that *that* had ever worked out for me before), now there were going to be people that hated me because of what I stood for - the law - and I was just going to have to get used to it.

***

It wasn't until the next day that I realised I could have arrested her for prostitution. *But I was off duty,* I told myself. Plus, if I really wanted to get information over the dead woman the last thing I needed to do was alienate the prostitutes in the area. This brought me to the question. Why did I want information on the dead woman? What was I going to do with it? Find the serial killer?

Well why not? A very small part of me asked.

Yeah right. There were experienced detectives working this case that were baffled, as if I could find anything useful. I slapped the small part of myself a few times till it shut up and then opened the manual.

I was nearly all the way through it and Bob had advised me as soon as I was finished I was going out on the beat with him. That news had given me much needed inspiration to keep reading. Daniel had finished his the day before and had disappeared that morning with Nathan. I had been green with envy, but Roger had turned up shortly afterwards and flirted with me which had placated me slightly, until I realised he'd dumped his dirty mug on my desk.

'Good work man.' Nathan's voice woke me from my doze.

What had I been doing? Oh yeah, right – reading that stupid manual.

'Thanks.' Daniel's voice sounded more embarrassed than normal.

I stood up and headed for the coffee machine. The sleepless nights were getting to me and I had high hopes for an apartment I was looking at after work today, but for right now, I needed caffeine.

Daniel and Nathan entered the muster room and sat down at their prospective desks to fill out paperwork. I made them both coffee and delivered it to them.

'How'd it go?' I asked Daniel, looking over his shoulder at the paperwork. It was an arrest report.

'Good.' He shrugged and smiled at me.

'He made his first arrest,' Nathan said.

'He did?' I felt the ugly green monster stirring inside me. 'That's great.' I wrestled the monster to the ground, slammed a lid over it and stuffed it into the back corner of my mind.

'Caught a shoplifter down at the 7-11.'

Damn, while I had been snoring, Daniel had been out arresting criminals. I really had to finish that manual.

I shuffled back to my desk and started reading again.

'How much do you have to go?' Bob asked me a few minutes later.

I showed him the book. 'Close enough, you can finish the rest tonight. Let's get out of here.'

I resisted the urge to throw my arms around his chubby frame as I jumped up from the desk and grabbed my things.

'What are we doing?' I asked him as we left the station.

'We're going to wander around and keep an eye on things.'

I was disappointed he hadn't said, 'We're going to kick some criminal arse,' or something to that effect. But truth be told, Bob didn't look like the type of policeman who ever kicked criminal arse. If he accidentally fell on one he would be sure to pin him down but I couldn't see him chasing anyone through the streets of King's Cross, or vaulting over a table to tackle the perpetrator like Daniel had apparently done.

It was a pleasant day to be wandering around and the pace Bob set allowed me to stare at the shiny, expensive clothing in the shop windows, but after a while I started to get bored so I began to play Roger's favourite game.

It was while Bob was buying himself a hot dog that I saw it.

A man stood in the park, the hood of his grey jumper pulled up over his head. As I watched, another untrustworthy looking character passed close by. I couldn't be sure, but it looked like something passed from one to the other.

I thought about it as we continued our rounds, suspicious about a couple of things. Firstly, obviously, the exchange, and secondly I found myself wondering why he was wearing a jumper in this temperature, with the hood pulled up. I mean I had a short sleeve shirt on and was glad I had put on my sports deodorant that morning. So when Bob went back for his second hotdog I stopped and watched.

The man was tall and skinny and had dark tufts of hair sticking out from under the hood of his jumper. His jeans had seen better days, more patches and frays obvious than whole denim. Wires traversed up the front of his jumper to his ears and he bobbed up and down, presumably to the music he was listening to. Either that or he was impersonating a cockatiel.

As I watched, a short plump man with a baseball cap pulled low walked right by him. Close enough to bump into him. Close enough to take something from him. This time I saw it clearly, the two hands smoothly passing objects one to the other, and before I had even thought about what I was doing I took off.

The tall man saw me coming and bolted. I could hear Bob shrieking my name from behind and a vision of him running - hotdog clasped in one hand, belly wobbling - made me want to turn to look, but I didn't. The man's legs were longer than mine and I couldn't afford to lose any ground.

We charged across the park and down the main street of King's Cross, his hoodie trailing out behind him like a flag. I dodged around a pedestrian and darted across the road after him through a break in the cars. He ran back up the hill towards the park and I could feel my breath coming in short, sharp jerks. He was getting away from me. I couldn't believe it, my first chase and he was going to get away.

Just as I was beginning to despair he raced around the corner back into the park and ran smack bang into Bob, who was bent over at the waist breathing heavily. The two of them went down, hard. I heard his head smack the pavement and winced. That was going to hurt later. Bob bounced and rolled, squishing his hotdog as he went.

I leapt over Bob, yanked my hand cuffs off my vest and secured the perpetrator's hands behind his back. I flashed him my badge, gave him my name and then read him his rights. I could hear a spatter of applause coming from a group of Japanese tourists standing at the edge of the park and resisted the urge to bow. Truth be told though, I was pretty impressed with myself.

'Blimey,' Bob said as he climbed to his feet. There was tomato sauce smeared over the front of his shirt and the hot dog sausage was sticking out of his top pocket. 'You showed him.'

'That's as far as you made it?' I asked. The hotdog vendor was barely 100 metres away.

'You seemed to have it covered.' He pulled the sausage out of his pocket, looked at it for a second and then took a bite.

'You're making a big mistake,' my captive said.

'You have the right to remain silent,' I reminded him.

'Don't say I didn't warn you.'

Holding onto the handcuffs firmly, I helped him to his feet. Bob and I shepherded him back to the police station.

Dave, who was currently the permanent front desk officer, nodded at us when we came through the front door. His eyebrows rose at the sight of our cuffed prisoner. 'What's he in for,' he asked.

'Drug dealing,' I said.

'I'll go get Richardson.'

We dragged our arrestee to an interview room, where he lounged on one of the chairs. His legs stretched out, his arms behind his head; he appeared to be quite at home. I could only assume it wasn't the first time he'd been brought in for questioning.

It wasn't long before Roger turned up. Like a puppy with a new toy, I was itching to show off my captive. *Oh boy.* I had it bad.

'Hey Trent,' he said, 'Dave said they'd brought you in. What were you thinking?'

'She's very perceptive,' he said, standing up and shaking Roger's hand.

'I was guessing it wasn't Bob,' Roger said, smiling at me.

Bob had the same look on his face that I was guessing was on mine. Utter confusion. At least I didn't have tomato sauce on mine.

'Bun, Bob, this is Detective Inspector Trent Bailey. He's working undercover here at the moment trying to bust a drug ring.'

Oh Fuck. I'd arrested an undercover police officer.

'I did try to warn you,' he said to me.

I seemed, for the first time in my life, to be unable to speak.

'Is she normally this quiet?' he asked Roger.

'No, not at all.'

'Her name's Bun?'

'That's my pet name for her; you know, cause of the hair.'

'Cute,' Trent said, looking me up and down.

'I *am* here,' I finally spluttered.

Trent chuckled and winked at me.

We left the two of them and proceeded back to our desks to write up the paperwork. I was feeling pretty deflated that all my work had come to zip. Plus, I had risked exposing an undercover operation. Still I couldn't help feeling mollified by the warm response Bob was getting to the story of my chasing Trent down. Nathan made him tell it twice, and then when Roger finally came back he got him to tell it again.

By then the tale, like all good stories, had improved, until I appeared to be almost superhuman in my pursuit of Trent.

If nothing else, working with Bob was going to make me look good.

***

Bruce was already there when I got to the park that night. Lancelot let out a bark when he saw Cocoa and then the two of them raced off together sniffing and weeing on everything they could.

'Good day?' Bruce asked as I took a seat beside him.

'Yes and no. You?'

'My day is just beginning.'

'What do you mean?' I asked.

He pulled a business card out of his pocket and handed it to me. It had the word Dazzle written across it in bold, hot pink writing and then an address. 'That's my club,' he said.

'Wow, you own a club?'

'You should come by and check it out.'

I looked at the brightly coloured card. 'You're open Wednesday to Sunday?'

'Uhuh, but the show doesn't start till ten.'

'Show?'

'We have a stage show. Singing and dancing, you know that sort of thing.'

'Sounds fun. I can't tonight.'

'School night?'

'Yeah, but maybe tomorrow night.' That was one of the nice things about being in the Police Force; we did four days on, four days off. After tomorrow I had four whole days to find a new apartment. Then I would do four night shifts before getting time off again.

'Well would you look at that,' Bruce said.

I glanced over at Lancelot and Cocoa, who had finished sniffing the grass and appeared to be more intent on sniffing each other.

'Puppy love,' Bruce squealed, clapping his hands together.

As we watched Lancelot mounted Cocoa and proceeded to hump him. Cocoa didn't seem to mind at all.

'Oh dear,' I said, jumping up to separate them. Bruce was laughing too hard to be of any help, but I finally managed to get them apart. Of course as soon as I let them go Cocoa decided it was his turn and leapt onto Lancelot, his little hips to-ing and fro-ing as he clutched the poodle with his front paws.

'Cocoa,' I said, shocked.

'Ohhh, that's so cute,' Bruce squealed.

Cute wasn't what I was thinking, but I held back. I really didn't want to offend my only friend in King's Cross. I finally separated them again and dragged them over to Bruce so he could hold onto Lancelot.

'I'd better get going anyway,' I said. 'Tomorrow?'

'Got a hot date before work.'

'Lucky you.'

'He's got a straight brother, maybe we could double some time.'

I laughed and said, 'Yeah maybe.'

Cocoa gave Lancelot one last look over his shoulder before allowing me to drag him back up the street.

'What were you thinking?' I asked him. 'And in public as well.'

Cocoa didn't feel the need to explain his actions as he trotted up the road, and I couldn't be mad. At least one of us had a boyfriend. That, of course, made me think of Roger. If the way he'd smiled at me when I'd left work that afternoon was any indication, hopefully soon I might have one too.

Chapter Seven

Sometimes My Mouth Gets Ahead Of My Brain

The last thing I expected when I got to work the next morning was to be dragged straight into Inspector Ramy's office.

'What the hell do you think you're playing at?' he said.

I stared at him, bewildered and wondering if he had the right person.

'Well don't just stand there.'

Should I jig up and down on the spot? Move from side to side? Maybe he was expecting me to break out into a Michael Jackson style moon dance. In the end I opted for the jigging.

He stared at me with wide eyes while I jigged. When he didn't say anything I threw some arms in, wiggling from side to side.

'What the bloody hell are you doing?' he finally spluttered.

'You told me not to just stand there,' I said.

'I want you to tell me what you were doing arresting Detective Inspector Bailey yesterday.'

So … the drug dealer I brought in from the street?' I said.

'Yes him.'

'So when I say the drug dealer I brought in from the street that's not giving you any insight into what I was thinking?'

'Don't get smart with me girl.'

'Not getting smart Sir.' I said. 'Just wondering how I was meant to tell he was an undercover policeman. Maybe you should make them wear a yellow ribbon or something.'

'A yellow ribbon?'

I winced and stepped back from the desk.

'A yellow ribbon? I've never heard of such a ridiculous idea.'

'It was a joke Sir.'

'You think almost blowing an undercover operation, months in the making, is a joke?'

'No Sir, the yellow…'

'I think you've had quite enough to say young lady. You can take this as your first formal warning on your probation. Another stunt like this and you'll be off the Force before you can even think about yellow ribbons. You're dismissed, *Probationary* Constable Smith.'

I turned and stalked to the door muttering under my breath.

'One more thing.'

I turned to look at him, trying to keep the look of distaste off my face.

'You'll be manning the front desk from now on.'

'But Sir,' I said, 'who'll make the men their coffee?'

He must have missed the sarcasm in my voice because he said, 'Oh, hmm, well I am sure they'll manage until you get back.'

I left his office, very proud of myself for not slamming the door, and made my way to the front desk.

'Anything I need to know?' I asked Dave.

'It's all in here,' he said, smiling as he thumped a huge manual.

'You are shitting me?' It was a different manual to the one I'd waded through already.

'Nope, get it read as fast as you can.'

I had a thought as I relieved him from the front counter. 'Hey Dave,' I said 'what did you do to get stuck out here.'

'Oh about nine months ago I went out on patrol and got caught having a nap in the park.'

'Nine months ago?' *Geez Louise.*

'Yeah,' he said with a big grin on his face, 'nine long months.'

***

'Work sucks,' I said to Cocoa when I got home. I lay on the couch with him curled up on my chest and told him all about it. He at least agreed with me that I had been treated in a most unfair manner.

The boys had been sympathetic. Nathan, Bob and Mark had bought me chocolate and Roger had come and hung around the front desk for a while trying to cheer me up.

'Bad luck bun,' I said, trying to imitate his posh English accent. It sounded so yummy when he'd said it.

Cocoa, bored with hearing me go on about Roger, jumped off my chest, padded to the door and whined.

'Sorry boy,' I said, getting up and grabbing his lead. I could do with some fresh air as well.

I took him down to the park and let him off, but we both agreed it was lonely there without Bruce and Lancelot, so after a few minutes I put him back on the lead and we went for a walk around the streets.

'Oh look,' I said to Cocoa, 'a dog groomers.'

I studied the photos of the dogs in the window and then took one of the business cards they had left in a holder out the front. Cocoa was going to need a grooming soon. His eyebrows were getting so long he could hardly see and his beard was matted.

As I slid the card into my pocket I felt another piece of cardboard. I pulled it out and looked at it. Dazzle. The trauma of the day had driven Bruce's club from my mind.

I thought about going to the club; imagining the music flowing around me as I sipped a cocktail and forgot all about Inspector Ramy, and all of a sudden I wanted to go. I hadn't been out forever, and I didn't feel like doing any study that night. This would be just what the doctor ordered – if he was a cute single doctor. And better yet I had the perfect outfit; a little black dress Becky had given me as a going away present. My mind made up, Cocoa and I headed for home.

***

A few hours later I hovered nervously outside Dazzle. It hadn't been hard to find; the pink neon sign flashed and danced in the dark. 'Come on Chanel,' I said, 'it's just a club.' Grasping the rail I descended carefully, making sure my fake Jimmy Choo shoes didn't catch on the stairs, and then I entered Dazzle.

There was music playing in the background, quiet enough that you could still have a conversation if you wanted. A large stage took up the entire far side of the club; the plush red curtain flowing to the floor. Small intimate tables were scattered around the rest of the room, their chairs positioned so each person could see the stage. Some of the tables were already occupied, the buzz of the conversation just audible over the music.

I headed for the bar and slid onto one of the stools, making sure my dress was pulled down over my thighs; nothing like an eye-full of hail damage to put off a prospective date.

Bruce was serving drinks at the other end of the bar. He bustled over to me, handing me a cocktail list.

'Hi,' I said, smiling at him.

He stared at me for a full second before squealing, 'Chanel, O M G girlfriend, you look amazing. Let me get a better look at you.' He flapped his hands at me, urging me to stand up.

I did, pirouetting on the spot before sitting back down; embarrassed but also secretly pleased to be getting some positive attention.

'Glam baby glam. I love your hair like that.'

I subconsciously patted my ponytail which was pulled up on top of my head. 'Thanks. How'd your date go?

He threw some ingredients in a blender, hit the switch for a few seconds and then emptied the contents into a glass which he deposited in front of me. Then he slithered out under a gap in the bar and took up a stool next to me. 'Wonderful,' he said, urging me with his hands to take a sip.

I did. It was delicious. 'What is this?' I said, holding up the glass to stare at the contents.

'House special, the Dazzle cocktail. You like?'

'I think I'm in love. Now tell me about your date.'

'Well he's H O T which is always a good start. And he's a doctor.'

'Wow, a hot doctor. I've been looking for one of them.'

'I'll keep my eyes out for you, but they're rare.'

'Maybe I should start hanging out around the emergency department.'

He let out a huge laugh, slapped me on the arm and then jumped off his stool. 'Oops, got a customer.'

The club was starting to get busier, about half of the tables were now full. I sipped my cocktail and people watched, noting that most of the couples appeared to be same sex. This was probably not the place I was going to meet the future Mr Smith. Hey, who was I kidding, I wasn't really looking for the future Mr Smith; I was looking for some fun.

The lights began to dim, the curtain rose, and I realised the show was starting. A long line of women were standing in a row, all of them tall and muscular. One of them moved to a microphone in the middle of the stage and started to sing; her deep voice soaring, her face melancholy. And then the music struck up, the song went from sad to cheerful and the rest of the women began to dance.

The show took my mind totally off work, but as soon as there was an interval, my thoughts returned to the scene in Ramy's office. What on earth had I been thinking when I'd suggested the yellow ribbons? I mean I wasn't serious obviously, but any idiot could see that the man had no sense of humour. I should have just shut up and taken it and then maybe I wouldn't be doomed to spend the rest of my life working the front desk.

A woman took a seat on the stool next to mine. 'The usual,' she said to Bruce. She had huge hair and lots of make-up; her lips were a deep shade of red. I recognised her as one of the women up on stage.

'I'm really enjoying the show,' I said to her.

She pivoted a little to look at me and held out her hand. 'Martine.'

I winced as I shook it - she was really strong. 'Chanel.'

'What's a cute little button of a thing like you doing in a bar by yourself?'

'I'm here with all my friends,' I said.

'Have they gone to the toilet?'

'No,' I said, shaking my head, 'meaning I have no friends. I just moved here.'

'What am I?' Bruce said from the other side of the bar. 'Pork chops?'

'You're the tastiest pork chop I've ever seen,' Martine said in her deep voice.

'I have no friends except for Bruce,' I amended.

'Well that's a sad state of affairs. We'll have to see what we can do about that.' Her smile was so sincere I thought, for a terrifying second, I was going to get all teary.

'Hey Ronnie,' she yelled, 'get over here.'

Another one of the showgirls wandered over to the bar and Bruce handed her a glass of wine. I recognised her as the singer. Up close she was even taller than she had appeared on stage. She wore a short leather skirt that emphasised her muscly legs and rock hard butt. I sighed. There wasn't the slightest hope my arse would ever be that good.

'This is Chanel,' Martine said.

'That's my favourite perfume.' Ronnie leant over and sniffed my neck. 'Yep, you smell good.'

'Ronnie,' Martine said, laughing as she slapped her friend on the arm. 'Don't freak her out. She's just a baby.'

'I gotta go anyway,' Ronnie said, winking at me. 'I'm up next.' She skolled the glass Bruce had handed her and strode off towards the stage.

'So what brings you to this neck of the woods?' Martine asked.

'Work,' I said with a sigh.

'What do you do for a crumb?'

'Don't hate me,' I said, looking at her, 'I'm a cop.'

'Wow. You don't look like a cop.'

'What do cops look like?'

'Well … bigger and burlier. And they have more facial hair.'

'I wax.'

'I wouldn't mind meeting a big burly hairy cop,' she said. 'Are there any where you work?'

I ran through the guys at work, trying to dissect out the burly hairy ones. Bob was pretty big, but he had a baby soft face, so I was guessing that didn't count. Plus he was more flab than fab, and I was thinking Martine was after fab.

'There's one,' I said, thinking of Roger, 'but he's not that hairy and I've got dibs on him.'

Martine let out a little squeal and clapped her hands together. 'Tell me all about him,' she said.

'He's blonde and really fit and well, he's English.'

'Say no more sister; nothing sexier than a man with an accent.'

'And he's a detective.'

'So he's successful as well. He sounds like the bomb.'

'He is pretty dreamy,' I said.

Bruce winked as he deposited another Dazzle house special in front of me. 'Ahh Martine,' he said, 'shouldn't you be getting ready?'

'Shit. Raincheck,' she said springing to her feet. 'I'm in the next act.'

The next act was a more upbeat number. They spun around on stage with umbrellas while Ronnie sang, 'It's Raining Men'. I found myself tapping my feet and bopping my head.

A few songs later, Martine reappeared by my side and took a seat. 'So,' she said, 'what happened at work today?' I looked at her in surprise and she said, 'You frown when you mention work.'

'Do you really want to hear it?'

'I'm done for the night so hit me.'

So I told her all about work and at the end she shook her head. 'That doesn't sound very fair. Isn't there a board or something you can complain to?'

'Probably,' I said, 'but from what I've learned of the Police Force, you don't want to create waves, especially not just out of the Academy. Plus ... I'm a woman.'

'Why should that make a difference?'

'Well, they recruited us pretty easily - part of the State Government's pledge to have more women on the Force. If I get known as a troublemaker I'll never get rid of the stigma.' I knew this from having listened to Rick talking. 'I just have to tough it out and earn their respect.' Unfortunately I had my doubts about whether or not it was possible for me to earn Inspector Ramy's respect; especially not after the yellow ribbon conversation.

'It's true,' she said, 'it's so easy for women to be accused of cashing in the furry chequebook.'

'Furry chequebook?'

'You know.' She pointed down to her nether regions.

I shook my head.

She rolled her eyes and pointed at her crutch.

'Oooh,' I said, 'the furry chequebook. I won't be using that.'

'Soooo what are you going to do?'

'Well...' A stupid idea had been rolling around in the back of my head but I was loath to voice it.

'You can tell me,' she said, shuffling closer.

Bruce handed me another drink. 'And me,' he said.

'Okay, but you can't tell anyone because it's silly.'

'Cross my heart,' Martine said.

'And hope to die,' Bruce finished.

'I want to find the serial killer.' I said the words in a rush, happy to have them out of my head and in the open. Once they were free they swirled around, taking form and becoming a reality.

My God, I really did want to find the serial killer. I hadn't admitted it even to myself. The idea was shocking and absurd, but it felt real to me. I wanted to hunt down the bastard who was doing those terrible things to women and make him pay. It didn't matter that they were prostitutes. They were people, with families and friends, and no-one deserved to be treated like that.

'Silly hey?' I said, looking at Bruce and Martine's shocked expressions.

'There's a serial killer?' Martine said.

'In the Cross?' Bruce added.

'You don't know?' How could they not know? It was five women now. I filled them in on the basics of the killings, leaving out anything I thought might be confidential.

'No wonder the girls have been acting so strangely,' Bruce said when I'd finished.

'The girls?' I asked.

'The group that work this area: Bianca, Rosie, Isabella and Lizette. 'They normally work different corners, but lately they've been hanging together.

'Huh. You know these girls?'

'They're friends,' Martine said.

'Do you think they'd talk to me?'

'If we introduced you, they might. They don't like pigs, sorry, cops much.'

I yawned and looked at my watch. It was already two in the morning. 'I need to get to sleep,' I said apologetically. 'I'm going to look at some apartments tomorrow.'

'Come back tomorrow night,' Martine said, 'and I'll see if I can get the girls to talk to you.'

'Thanks.' I gave her a hug, surprised at how muscly her torso was. She must really work out.

I walked the short distance home with my mace in one hand and a whistle in the other, determined not to become victim number six. But even though I was scared I was also euphoric. I had my first lead. Tomorrow night I was going to get to talk to some of the Cross's prostitutes. I just hoped they could give me some useful information.

***

I looked at three apartments that day. All as bad, if not worse, as the one I was currently living in. I wasn't really asking for much. It didn't matter if it wasn't modern. I just wanted a clean, quiet place to live. The rest I could deal with.

I did, however, drop into the dog groomers and get Cocoa booked in for the next day. I also did a large amount of window shopping, too scared to enter the shops in case I damaged the shiny fabrics.

If I knew one thing it was that I couldn't afford anything in those designer stores.

The show was in full swing by the time I got to Dazzle that night. Bruce was busy with a large group of Asian tourists so I took my seat at the bar and tried to pick Martine out of the dancers.

Eventually Bruce finished and came over to greet me.

'Lizette and Rosie have agreed to come here and talk to you,' he said.

'Really?' Raw excitement zinged through my veins.

'Couldn't pin them down to a time,' he said, 'they'll be here in between business.'

I sipped my cocktail while I thought about that. I was going to interview them knowing they had just had sex with a strange man. I hadn't realised what a prude I was till that flashed through my head. I blamed my Mum for my prudish side, always harping on about my virtue and reputation. But Mum was old before her time and I swore I wasn't going to be like that, so I pushed the thought away and focused instead on what I wanted to ask them.

Lizette and Rosie approached the bar about an hour later. They were pretty girls, one plump and one thin. They both wore short skirts and tops with plunging necklines, revealing an ample amount of cleavage. Lizette was chewing gum in a quick, anxious fashion, her eyes darting nervously around the room.

After Bruce introduced us they perched on the edge of the stools closest to me, their bodies tensed as if ready to flee. Rosie kept looking over her shoulder and licking her lips.

'Thank you for coming,' I said.

Lizette blew a large bubble, popped it with her finger and then stabbed the gum back into her mouth.

'So, umm, I was wondering if you knew anything about the latest murder?' It wasn't how I had wanted to start the questioning but their body language was unnerving me.

'And if we did, why should we tell you?' Lizette asked. She blew out another bubble which swiftly met the same fate as the first.

'Because you care that prostitutes are dying? Yeah right,' Rosie said. She blinked rapidly a few times and then rubbed the back of her neck.

'I care that *people* are dying,' I said, staring into her eyes. She met my gaze for a few seconds before breaking away and looking nervously over her shoulder. I resisted the urge to do the same.

Lizette gnawed at her bottom lip as she stared at the floor. 'Maybe you do,' she said, scraping her hands through her hair. 'But how do we know we can trust you?'

'Do you know something?' I leant forward in my chair.

Like a startled animal she slid off the stool and backed away from me. 'I don't think you can help us,' she said, shaking her head. 'You're too young and ...'

'Powerless,' Rosie said, also standing up.

'You do know something,' I said. 'You have to tell me what you know.'

'I don't think so,' Rosie said. 'We don't know who sent you.' She took Lizette's hand and they hurried from the room.

'That was weird,' I said to Bruce once they'd gone.

'Did they tell you anything?'

'No, but they know something. They're scared.'

'Wouldn't you be?'

'Yes, but it's more than that.' I paused to think about it. 'They wanted to be protected and they didn't think I was up to the job. They were right too. I mean what could I do for them?' I felt deflated. I'd been so excited about this, certain I'd get a lead, and I still had nothing.

'What are you going to do?' Bruce asked.

'What can I do?'

'Don't give up.'

'Well, I guess I could go over the crime scenes and see if they missed anything.' I snorted as I said it. I mean as if I would find something that the trained detectives had missed, that *Roger* had missed. I may as well be looking for the cure for cancer.

Plus, I only knew of the one site, so I was going to have to wheedle the others out of Roger. I was going to have to bat my eyelids and flirt with everything I had.

Well, *that* I could do.

I had no doubt that with my kissaliscious bubble gum lip gloss, school-girl-cute-ponytail, trusty push-up bra, and a 'lost' button on the top of my uniform blouse, that I would have the information I needed by the end of my first day back at work.

Chapter Eight

Sherlock Holmes
Eat Your Heart Out

I woke with just enough time to scoff a bagel and get Cocoa to the groomers. It was a beautiful day, the sort on which you couldn't help but feel good, no matter how much your life sucked. I decided to walk down into town around the harbour and through the Botanical Gardens while Cocoa was being buffed and polished.

I took my time making my way to the harbour. Once there I found a café with a view of the city and ordered a coffee. Sydney really was beautiful. I just wished I could find some decent accommodation I could afford.

Those thoughts were bouncing around in my head when my phone rang. It was Martine.

'Hey girlfriend, where are you at?'

'I've walked into town,' I said. 'What's up?'

'You won't believe it; I bumped into the guy who owns the apartment block I live in.'

'He owns the whole block?'

'Yes, but I wouldn't go there: short, fat, small man syndrome. Anyway it turns out there's an apartment up for rent and I told him about you.'

'Are dogs allowed?'

'Not normally, but I told him about how you're a cop, and Cocoa's gone through police dog training...'

'You know that's not strictly true, right?' The night before I'd told her and Bruce about the farting incident.

'Of course, but *he* doesn't. Then I started talking about all the killings and how nice it would be to have a police dog on the premises. How it would give all the tenants peace of mind and let us stop thinking about moving out of the Cross.'

'*Martine.*' I had to laugh at her audacity.

'Anyway, he wants to meet you and Cocoa this afternoon and if he's happy it's yours at a discounted price.'

'Really?' I screeched into the phone.

'Ouch.'

'Sorry.' I lowered my voice and smiled at the people who had turned to look at me. 'What time?'

'He'll be there painting the apartment till four.'

'Cocoa's at the groomers, I have to get him at 3.30,' I said.

'The one around the corner from Dazzle?'

'Yep.'
'I'll meet you there.'

***

Martine was waiting out the front when I arrived at the groomers.

'We have to hurry or we'll miss him,' she said. Even at this time of day her auburn hair was enormous and she was sporting a full face of make-up. I felt extremely under-dressed in my walking shorts and shoes.

Cocoa was in a pen playing with a few other dogs. When he saw me he started barking and jumping up and down. His clip looked good and his beard was full and fluffy but his toenails were painted hot pink.

'Holy moly,' Martine said, staring at his feet. They had clipped them short like a poodle to emphasise his nails.

The groomer released him from the pen and he bounded towards us, barking as he leapt into my arms. He proceeded to give me a full face wash, managing to get his tongue into my mouth twice as I struggled to avoid him.

'That is one of the most disturbing things I have ever seen,' Martine said.

'Don't knock it, it's the most action I've had this year.' I looked down at his toes. They looked ridiculous. 'We don't have time to have this removed do we?'

She looked at her watch. 'Not if you want to see the apartment.'

I paid the groomer and put Cocoa's hot pink collar back on. It and the lead perfectly matched his toenails. The groomer nodded her head in satisfaction.

Martine shook hers and sighed.

We made it with five minutes to spare. Joe, the landlord, had finished painting and was cleaning up his mess. The apartment wasn't huge, but it was clean and bright with a modern kitchen and bathroom, and a huge window in the living room looking out towards the city. The bedroom was on a mezzanine platform looking over the living area. I loved it.

'I thoughts you said he was a police dog,' Joe said to Martine. His paunch was flowing over the top of his workpants and I was having trouble not looking. Unfortunately the alternative was his chest, where his half open shirt revealed several dangling gold chains and a large amount of sweaty black hair.

'Oh he is,' she said. 'He's undercover.'

He looked sceptical so I said, 'Look we can't give you all the details. That's why they call it undercover. But let's just say he's trained to sniff out explosives.'

I was going to say drugs, but at the last second considered the fact that Joe may not want a dog that can sniff out drugs living in his block. If I had seen Joe while out with Roger I would have guessed drug dealer or pimp.

'Oh,' he said, 'like one of them dogs that finds terrorists?'

I didn't say anything, but I tapped the side of my nose and nodded.

'You can't tell anyone,' Martine warned him.

'Don't want to blow his cover,' I said, smiling sweetly.

Joe looked at Cocoa with a look bordering on reverence. 'It would be a pleasure to have you living in my apartment,' he told me.

I tried to conceal my excitement. 'When can we move in?'

'Well the paint should be dry by tomorrow. Do you want it furnished? Cause it'll take me a couple of days to lose the furniture.'

'Furnished will be perfect.'

'Well tomorrow then. I can meet you here at say nine and give you the keys.'

I contemplated my week while I painted my toes the same colour as Cocoa's (if you can't beat 'em join 'em). Sure there had been some shitty stuff that had happened but it was easily overshadowed by my new friends and apartment. Tomorrow I would move and then on Monday I would tease the location of the other murder scenes out of Roger.

I rang Mum and filled her in on my week, leaving out the grisly details of the body we had found and the fact that I was going to try to single-handedly track down a dangerous serial killer, and then I went to bed.

***

The one day I really wanted to see Roger and he still hadn't shown up for work. All right, so I really wanted to see him every day, but today was different. Today it wasn't about my Guinness Book of Records' sized crush.

Because I was doing the early night shift there were only a few hours that we overlapped, and that time was ticking away. I was kept busy with a stream of visitors coming through the front door: people bailing out friends or relatives, officers bringing in suspects for interviews and building contractors. One of the rooms had sustained some rain damage a few months ago and it was only now being fixed.

When he finally did show it was with a woman in handcuffs. Her attire indicated she was one of the working girls; bright red tight spandex skirt and boob tube top. It was a brave clothing choice given her bootaliscious butt and impressive chest.

'Hey girlfriend,' she said to me as he dragged her through the front doors. She didn't seem at all concerned about her predicament.

'Bianca,' Roger said, 'can I trust you to stay here or do I have to lock you up?'

'You can trust me,' she said, shooting him a cheeky grin. Her large teeth shone white against the glowing ebony of her skin. I found myself responding to her cheery disposition. It was either that or the fact that Roger was in the same room with me.

As soon as Roger left, Bianca bolted for the front door. I vaulted over the counter, a feat that surprised me as much as it did her, and landed in front of the doors. It seemed all the obstacle course training had paid off.

'Don't even think about it,' I said.

'Damn girl, you like a superwoman or something?'

I shook my head at her and pointed to the chairs on the other side of the room.

'You been exposed to some serious radiation shit?'

'No,' I said, laughing as I made my way back round to the other side of the table.

'You're like a ninja, right? I bet you could kick my big black arse all over this city.'

'Who could kick your arse?' Roger asked.

'Your girl there. She's scary.'

'Chanel? Yes, she is scary.' He shot me a grin that threatened to stop my heart.

I took a deep breath and tried to get a grip on my emotions. I wasn't going to look so tough if I started hyperventilating just because he'd smiled at me.

It wasn't so much that he'd smiled. It was the way he'd smiled, and I don't want to bore you, but it was cheeky and endearing and there had been a light in his eyes when he'd said my name. I'd had to stop myself vaulting the table again so I could wrap myself around him and shove my tongue down his throat.

I tore my eyes away and focused on the stupid manual I was only part of the way through, while I tried to think of a way to swing the conversation the way I wanted it to go. I couldn't do it with Bianca in the room though so I was going to have to wait for him to finish with her.

As Bianca followed him into the interview room something tickled at the back of my mind. I ignored it, knowing if I tried to identify what it was it would slip further from my conscious mind. Eventually it surfaced, floating up to bob amongst my other thoughts.

Hadn't Bruce said that one of the working girls they were friends with was a Bianca? I wondered if it was the same one. I tried to suppress my excitement but by the time Roger had finished with his interview I was almost hopping from foot to foot.

'What are you in for?' I asked her, smiling in my friendliest manner.

'I had some Buddha on me.'

'Buddha?'

'Some Maryjane?'

I shrugged my shoulders.

'Some gangster? Locoweed? Ganja? A reefer?'

I shook my head as I stared at her and wondered what the hell she was on about.

'Some grass.'

'Oh marijuana,' I said.

'You're as white as your skin. No wonder you a cop.'

'I've tried it,' I said before I remembered where I was. I shot a nervous look over my shoulder. 'Once,' I whispered.

She chuckled and shook her head.

'Are you a friend of Bruce's?' I said.

'Dazzle Bruce?'

'Yep that one.'

'He's the bomb,' she said. 'He don't care what the colour of your skin is or what you do for dough.'

Roger appeared at the front office door and I stopped my line of questioning.

'You still here?' he said to Bianca over the counter.

'I'm just chatting to your super girl. She's a blast. But I'm going now.'

Roger came into the front office as she pushed out through the front door and sashayed her way up the steps, an impressive amount of thigh hanging out the bottom of her skirt.

'So Roger,' I said, turning to face him. I hadn't realised how close he was standing and I found myself staring up into his blistering blue eyes. I immediately lost my train of thought.

'Yes Chanel,' he said, smiling down at me.

I'd spent hours fantasising about being this close to him and now that it was happening I hadn't the faintest idea what to do. 'I was thinking,' I said, stalling for time as I tried to remember what the hell I had been thinking.

'So have I,' he said.

Dear God. My heart was racing, my palms were sweating and my knees were trembling.

'You go first,' I said, hoping he was thinking what I was thinking.

'I was wondering if I could have my foot back?'

I looked down to see that one of my feet was squishing the toe of his boot.

'Sorry,' I said, jumping away from him.

I heard someone clearing their throat from behind me. It was Bianca.

'I think I left my sunglasses in that room,' she said to Roger.

After he had left to look for them she said to me, 'Dang girl, you work fast. I sure am sorry about my timing.'

'Not at all,' I said, 'we were discussing a case.'

'Uhuh. I'm sure you were. He's a fine package. I wouldn't mind discussing his case.'

'Shhh,' I said, as Bob and Nathan came down the stairs.

'Yes sirree, the way his ass moves in those uniform pants, well it's enough to make a girl lie down and beg.'

'Shut *up*,' I hissed under my breath as they passed the counter, heading for the back offices.

Roger returned with a pair of red sunglasses which he handed to Bianca. 'Thank you kind sir,' she purred. 'Might see you later at Dazzle,' she said and then she winked and left the building.

'Dazzle?' Roger asked.

'Hmmm? I have no idea what she's talking about.'

'You wanted to ask me something?'

'Actually,' I said, moving to the other side of the office. I was working on the principle that if I kept enough space between us my brain might still work. 'I've been thinking about that woman we found.'

'What about her?'

'Well I was thinking about all of them,' I said. 'Were they all killed in the same alley?' Oh yeah, nice work Chanel. That sure was a subtle and tricky line of questioning. There was no way he would see where *that* was going.

'No,' he said. 'If they were we could post a guard on it, or put security cameras in to catch the bastard.' I was surprised by the vehemence in his voice. 'Why do you ask?' he said, staring into my eyes again.

'I was... ummm...just interested.' Christ when he gazed at me like that I felt like a space ship caught in a tractor beam.

'Why don't you check out the case board?' he said.

'Pardon?'

'The case board for the Cross serial killer - it's out the back.'

'Right,' I said, 'case board.'

At the end of my shift I went out to the back office to get my handbag and found the case board. It was behind Roger's desk, so I was surprised I hadn't noticed it before. I had spent an inordinate amount of time staring at his desk when I had been out the back. But then I had been staring at him, not his surroundings.

There was a map of King's Cross with pins marking the sites the bodies had been found. I jotted them down into my notebook while also looking nervously over my shoulder, and then I bolted out into the night.

***

The next morning I packed some ziplock plastic bags in my handbag and headed down the apartment building stairs going over my plan in my head. I was going to go to the lane in which we found Leticia first. Her name had been listed on the case board and it was nice to finally have a name for her. I had felt disrespectful thinking of her as 'that woman' or 'the body'.

I had just reached the ground floor when I remembered I had forgotten to pack rubber gloves.

Sighing, I turned to start the trek back upstairs and ran into a tall man wearing a brown suit.

'Sorry,' I said. What sort of policewoman was I? I hadn't even heard anyone behind me.

'That's okay Chanel,' he said in a monotone voice.

I peered up at him. 'Do I know you?' I asked. He looked vaguely familiar.

'Yes,' he said in that same dead tone.

I stared at him for a while, trying to work out where I'd met him.

He sighed and then gestured at himself. 'I'm Marty,' he said. When I didn't say anything he sighed again and in a very familiar voice said, 'Chanel, it's Martine.'

'Jesus,' I said, jumping backwards. The face was the same, but that is where the similarities ended. Where Martine was vital and alive, Marty seemed dead. He appeared miserable in his boring suit and plain shoes.

'You're bald?' I said.

'I shave. It's easier with the wigs.'

'So you're a …..' I was going to say man, but that was obvious and didn't really sum it up.

'An accountant.'

'Not quite what I meant,' I said.

'Oh… I'm a drag queen.'

I stared at him for a while, trying to correlate this person with my Martine. I couldn't do it. 'So Ronnie?'

'Yes he is too.'

'And Bernadette?'

'We all are. I'm surprised you didn't work it out before.'

'I'm from Hickery,' I said, as if that could explain how naïve I was.

We stood and stared at each other for a few more seconds and then I said, 'I've got to get some rubber gloves.'

'Oh looking for evidence?' It was hard to tell if he was interested when he said it in that dull voice.

'Ahuh. Maybe I'll come by and see you after work tonight?'

'That would be nice,' he said.

I moved to the side so he could get past me and watched him shuffle up the street. It was unbelievable to think that that sad man, who appeared barely able to put one foot in front of the other, could dance the Cancan in five inch heels.

***

The lane had been scary when I had followed Roger that day; by myself it was terrifying. My mind played tricks on me, visualising shapes in the shadows, imagining the killer stalking behind me. By the time I got to the end I was exhausted with fear. I took a few moments to steady myself, deep breathing as I fought the urge to run back down the alley. But then I remembered Leticia, and I started to search.

I had no idea what I was looking for. I was just hoping the investigators had missed something that I wouldn't. I mean it really was a long shot, but it was the only shot I had.

Her blood was still visible in the dirt of the alley; a blackened stain of pain and misery. I stared at it and tried to imagine what it would have felt like to have my life leaking out of me, to know I was going to die.

And that was when I saw it. A cigarette butt ground into the dirt so it was barely visible.

I put on a rubber glove and picked up the butt, holding it up for inspection. It didn't look like a normal cigarette butt: the colour was almost black. I placed it in a plastic bag and tucked it into my pocket. Another few minutes revealed nothing else unusual. There was some rubbish lying around, a few cans and an old newspaper, but I doubted very much that he had stopped to eat a can of spaghetti or read the newspaper after he had killed her. But have a cigarette? Well that I could imagine.

I debated showing it to Roger, but decided against it. Firstly, I had no proof it was the killer's; I needed to look at the other sites first, and secondly I had already had a formal warning. If word got back to Ramy that I had become a solo investigator I would probably spend the rest of my life manning the front desk - that was if I didn't get kicked off the Force first.

The second site wasn't as creepy. The alley was shorter and not so dark, but it was in a more secluded area of the Cross. I scoured the area, but found nothing. By the time I had found nothing at the next three locations I was starting to feel pretty stupid.

I mean what did I think I was doing? It wasn't like I had known the women who had been killed.

But then Leticia's bloody face flashed into my mind.

That could have been my Mum. Hell, it could have been me. It was only luck that separated that woman's fate from all the other women living in this area. While the killer walked free we were playing Russian roulette every time we left home. And I didn't want to live in a world where our hold on life was so tentative and do nothing about it.

I spent more time at the last site, not wanting to give up without finding my matching clue. I was pretty certain I was in the right spot; the case board had had photos of the bodies and the surrounding area. But even after I had moved all the rubbish out of the way, bits of paper that might have blown in over the site, I didn't find it.

I was feeling pretty despondent having just wasted my morning off on an ego-fuelled goose chase. Pulling the plastic bag out of my pocket I walked over to a dumpster and started to lift the lid. I froze. Resting on the very edge of the lid was a perfectly matched butt.

My excitement threatening to overflow, I placed it carefully in a second bag and marked the location on the plastic, and then I went back to the other sites. Before I had been looking at the ground, now I was looking everywhere. And I found them. Strategically placed behind a down pipe, under a bin, on top of an awning; there was a butt at each of the locations a body had been found.

Perhaps it was a common brand of cigarette, but if that was the case why was there only one at each site? There was a good chance there was some saliva on them, which meant DNA. But what if it was somebody without a prior conviction?

I thought about it all that night at work, while also wrangling with the desire to share my find with Roger. But the fear of getting dragged into Ramy's office won over that desire to share and I decided to keep it to myself until I had some more concrete proof.

***

I knocked off work at three in the morning and decided to drop into Dazzle. I still hadn't recovered from my shock of meeting Marty and had decided the best way to deal with it was to imagine that Martine and Marty were two different people.

Martine sat with Bruce and Ronnie and a couple of the other girls around a table. Bruce had some paper and a pen and was taking notes.

'What's going on?' I asked.

'We're planning a new routine.'

Martine waved at me from the other side of the table. She looked nervous and I felt bad for making her feel that way.

'Why don't you have a seat at the bar? We're finished for tonight,' Bruce said. 'We've just been arguing about whether or not to hire a choreographer, but we can't afford it.'

'Why do you need one? Your other routines look great,' I said, pulling out a barstool.

'Yes, but we stole them from movies,' Martine said. She pulled a chair out next to me. 'So how did you go today?'

I looked over my shoulder to see if anyone was listening. 'Good,' I said once I'd made sure no-one could overhear us.

I told her of my find and my indecision over what to do with it.

'Why don't you take them to the tobacconist on Fleming St and see what brand they are?' she suggested. 'If they are as unusual as you think, there might be a limited number of users in the area.'

I could have leapt out of my chair and kissed her, and I was considering doing it when I heard a familiar voice. 'Hey super girl, you didn't tell me you knew Martine.'

Bianca was wearing a bright orange, lycra dress, which stretched heroically over her curves and revealed an ample amount of cleavage.

'She's my best friend in Sydney,' I said.

'What about me?' Bruce said as he wiggled out from under the bar.

'You're my best dog walking friend,' I said.

He laughed and then air kissed Bianca. 'What brings you here gorgeous?'

'I'm looking for Rosie and Lizette. Have you seen them?'

'Not for a few days,' he said.

Bianca sighed and frowned; the expression didn't look right on her.

'I wouldn't worry honey,' Martine said, 'you know they'll show up eventually.'

'Yeah you're right,' Bianca said. 'But I worry about them when they go on a drug binge.'

'Do you think that's what they're doing?' I asked.

'Not seeing as how you're a big tough policewoman,' she said. 'Those girls are as clean as fresh snow. No drugs have ever entered their pure little bodies.'

I laughed and held my hands out. 'I'm off duty,' I said. Besides, it wasn't the users I was interested in, it was the dealers.

'They'll probably be back tomorrow,' Bruce said.

She blew out a big puff of air, still looking worried. 'Oh well, I better go earn the rent,' she finally said. She blew us all kisses before leaving the bar.

I had wanted to talk to her about the killings, but it was apparent from her body language that whatever it was that had Lizette and Rosie scared stupid, she didn't know about it.

Martine gave me directions to the tobacconist, which was just up the road from work, and I left soon after, keen to get home to Cocoa and my bed.

The red light on my answering machine was flashing when I got in. It was a message from Mum telling me she was coming to visit and giving me the details of the train she would be on in a couple of days' time. I wasn't sure I wanted her to come while the killer was still on the loose, but then I didn't want to tell her that because then she'd be worried about me. In the end I figured she wouldn't be going out after dark unless she was with me anyway so I needn't worry.

I entered the details of her train in my phone and then I crawled into bed.

***

I was waiting impatiently outside the tobacconist when he opened at nine-thirty the next morning. I had arrived there fifteen minutes earlier and spent the wait fretting over what to say. I didn't want news of what I was doing to get around, certainly not back to the police station or, even worse, the killer.

'Hello love,' he said as he pushed up the shutters. His forehead was already covered in a fine mist of perspiration. It was going to be a hot day.

I followed him into the shop and looked around. All of the cigarettes were behind the counter, in line with government regulations. The rest of the shop was filled with Darrel Lea chocolates. I amused myself by picking out some rocky road; putting off the awkward conversation for as long as possible.

'I was wondering if you could help me,' I finally said, pulling out a plastic bag with a butt in it. I handed him the bag and said, 'Could you tell me what type of cigarette this is from?'

'That's not a cigarette,' he said, 'it's a cigar.'

'But it's so thin.'

'Not all cigars are the big thick type.' He opened a cupboard under the counter and pulled out a box of thin dark brown cigars. There was a picture of a woman in a grass skirt and bikini on the front.

'Hula girl?' I said.

He placed a few more packets on the counter, each slightly different from the last.

'Vanilla, mango, chocolate, coconut,' I said, reading the packets.

I looked at the cigars through the cellophane wrapping on the box. The end was identical to the ones I had found. A surge of triumph burnt through my chest.

'Do many people smoke these?' I said.

'Flavoured cigars?' He scratched the tuft of hair on his chin and cocked his head to the side.

'They're a bit of an acquired taste. The coconut ones seem to be the most popular.'

'Could you tell which flavour this one is?' I asked.

'I'd have to light it.'

I thought about it for a second, quickly discarding the idea. Lighting it would potentially destroy any DNA and probably wouldn't give me any useful information. For all I knew every butt was a different flavour.

I paused while I considered my next move. 'So do you think it would be possible to get a list of the people who buy them regularly?' I asked.

'Who's asking?'

His face had hardened and I gulped as I pulled my badge out of my handbag and showed it to him. 'Probationary Constable Smith,' I said.

'Well Probationary Constable Smith,' he said, almost spitting out the probationary, 'I think if people want to smoke flavoured cigars, then they have the right to do that.'

'Yes of course they do,' I said. 'It's just... well... you could help solve a case.' I was hoping he had played cops and robbers when he was a little boy and was left with the yearning to be a policeman.

'And I could alienate my clients,' he said. I was guessing that was a no on the cops and robbers.

'Surely they would understand,' I said, smiling sweetly.

'Understand that I'd sold them out?' He scratched his beard again and I thought I saw something scurrying out of the way of his fingers. It looked like a flea. 'Are you going to buy that?' he said, pointing to the rocky road, 'cause if you're not a customer I'm going to have to ask you to clear out.'

I thought about not buying it out of spite, but I've never been a spiteful person, and besides, now I had a real craving for it. I passed him the money and then placed it in my handbag thinking hard of some other way to convince him. In the end I realised the only way to do it was to get a search warrant. I was going to have to pass the evidence over to Roger and let him deal with it.

I left the shop, stopping to open the rocky road and stuff a piece of it into my mouth. The marshmallow and smooth chocolate helped a little but I still had an urge to cry. I wanted to cry for the dead women and cry because I was lonely and cry because it was that time of the month. But most of all I wanted to cry because even though I had succeeded I had failed. I was going to have to risk exposure to hand over the evidence, but the alternative was to allow more deaths to occur. I felt hopeless and helpless but I knew one thing. I couldn't live with myself if I let someone die for my own selfish needs.

I stuffed more chocolate into my mouth and then I went home to get ready for work.

***

My feeling of misery lasted right up till about three minutes after I got to work when it spiralled into something far worse. I was desperately hoping that Roger would be there so I could give him the evidence in private. He wasn't, but the paperwork scattered over his table told me that he hadn't finished for the day.

I glanced up at the case board and stiffened in horror. Leticia's photo had been the last one when I'd left to go home that morning. It wasn't anymore. The new photo showed a woman slumped next to a dumpster. Her front was covered in blood from the tell-tale neck wound. Even though her eyes were glassy, her skin pale, I recognised her.

When Bianca had been searching for Rosie and Lizette last night, I now knew where Rosie had been.

Tears clouded my vision and I turned and ran smack bang into Roger's chest.

'Sorry,' I sobbed, trying to get around him to the sanctity of the toilet.

'Hey,' he said, 'what's up?'

I nodded my head at the board as tears streaked down my face. 'I knew her,' I said. 'Well met her,' I corrected, hiccupping and sobbing.

He pulled me into him and put his arms around me, rocking me while I cried. I put my face into his chest and snuggled into him, partly because it felt so damned nice, and partly to hide my face. I'd never been a pretty crier, and I knew that at that moment, my eyes would be red and puffy and my nose would be running.

The thought of getting snot on his shirt made me jump back and wipe my eyes. I dug around in my handbag for a tissue and came across the sealed plastic bags containing the butts. I handed him the bags and then blew my nose, trying to sound delicate and feminine. I sounded, instead, a bit like the lead horn in a brass band.

'What's this?' he said when I had finished warming up my trumpet.

'I found them at the murder sites,' I said.

'The murder sites?'

'Yesterday,' I said. 'I found one at each of the sites a body was found.' I was hoping he wasn't going to be too angry.

He looked at the bags one by one, holding them up to get a better view.

'What do you think they are?' he said.

I was guessing that was a rhetorical question. 'I think the killer smoked one every time he made a kill.'

'But they could be anyone's cigarettes.'

'They're not,' I said. 'They're Hula Girl Flavoured Cigars. The probability of there being one at each site is a billion to one.'

He raised his eyebrows and smiled.

'Give or take a few million,' I added.

'I tell you what,' he said, 'tomorrow I'll have a look at the new site and if I find one I'll enter them all as evidence and go talk to the tobacconist up the road.'

'You'll need a search warrant.' I could feel myself blush as I said it.

He shook his head. 'What are we going to do with you?'

'Spank me,' I thought, but what I said was, 'Please don't tell Ramy.'

He looked thoughtful, 'So even if this helps break the case you don't want him to know it was you?'

'If it breaks the case I'm hoping he'll retract the formal warning. If it doesn't I'd prefer he not know. He'd probably find a reason to give me another warning.

He sighed. 'I didn't think the way he treated you was very fair; if anything Trent should have been reprimanded for being spotted.'

It felt good to have him defend me, even if it was in private.

'All right I won't tell Ramy, but I'll see what I can do about the front desk.'

I could have thrown my arms around his neck and kissed him, and that was before he'd promised to help me. Now I was ready to carry his first-born child.

Chapter Nine

Alright – Who Stole My Mother?

I picked Mum up from the train station the following evening. It took both of us to carry all her luggage to the car.

'Geez,' I said, as I struggled to load her enormous suitcase into the boot, 'how long are you visiting?'

'Well,' she said, 'the thing is I'm thinking of staying.'

I almost dropped her vanity bag in shock. Mum living in the big city? Mum, who had always preached about the peace and quiet of the country, giving it all up? My prudish, old-before-her-time mother, rubbing shoulders with my gay and drag queen friends? It didn't bear thinking about.

'Ahh Mum,' I said, 'King's Cross is pretty full on.'

'Bring it on,' she said as she hopped into the passenger seat.

Bring it on? I mouthed. What the hell had happened to my Mother?

'But won't you miss all your friends?'

'There's always the phone,' she said. 'Oh and I've got an email account now.'

It took us a couple of trips to get all of Mum's stuff from the underground parking area up to the apartment, where it crowded my small living area. Mum was going to be sleeping on the sofa-bed, and I wasn't sure how long it was going to work if she did indeed stay.

'Did I mention it only has one bedroom?' I said.

'Oh it will do just fine until I find a place of my own.'

'Wow,' I said, 'you've really thought this through.'

'You're not the only one who got bored with Hickery. Speaking of which, have you heard from Becky?' She opened the fridge, pulled out a bottle of wine out and poured some into a couple of glasses she found in a cupboard.

'Mum,' I said as she took her first sip, 'you don't drink.'

'What ever gave you that idea?'

She handed me a glass and I took a huge gulp as I sat down on the couch. 'Becky's good. They're working in Kalgoorlie.' I took another sip of my wine before saying, 'What are you planning to do for work?'

The words were just out of my mouth when there was a knock on the door. I opened it to find Martine with a bottle of bubbly in her hand.

'I heard about Rosie,' she said.

'Martine,' I said, raising my eyebrows, 'meet my Mum.' I hoped she'd get the hint. I didn't want to freak Mum out just yet.

She nodded her head slightly and I moved aside to let her in. Bouncing straight over to Mum she held out her hand and said, 'I'm Martine. So pleased to meet you Mrs Smith.'

'Call me Lorraine,' Mum said.

I glanced between the two of them. In truth they were far closer in age than Martine and I were. Mum had popped me out at the tender age of 19, so she'd celebrated her 40th when I'd had my 21st.

I pulled the cork on the bubbly while they chatted, desperately trying to put a finger on the change in Mum. The problem was that my fingers just weren't big enough. The changes in Mum were huge. When I'd left Hickery her favourite words had been 'swear jar', now she was letting fly with language so colourful even I didn't use it, and when she dropped the 'F' bomb I almost dropped a glass.

'Jesus,' I said, waiting for her to say, 'swear jar', but she didn't even break stride in her rendition of being mugged and hit by a car.

'Chanel never told me what a hoot you are,' Martine said.

'That's because I didn't know she was a hoot,' I said, standing in the door to the lounge room.

'Now now Chanel,' she said, hopping up and relinquishing the glasses from me, 'someone had to set a good example for you.' She handed Martine a glass and took a seat beside her. 'Although even with that good example I did wonder.' She put her glass on the coffee table and pulled out a packet of cigarettes.

'You smoke?' I felt like I was in an alien body-swap movie.

She paused in the act of lighting up and raised an eyebrow at me.

'Not in here,' I informed her.

'Spoil sport.'

'You can smoke at the club,' Martine said.

'Club?'

'Where I work. We do a show each night. You should come down and check it out.'

'A show?' Mum said.

'We dance and sing.'

'Sounds fun. Chanel?' Mum said.

'We can go tonight.' I was surprised she'd even thought to ask me.

As Mum and I were getting ready to go to Dazzle I said, 'Hey Mum there's something you should know about Martine.' I wasn't sure if I was trying to prepare her or shock her.

'Apart from the fact she's a drag queen?'

I stopped putting on my lipstick and turned to stare at her. 'You knew?'

'Honey... she's got size thirteen feet and an Adam's apple. What's not to know?' She smoothed her skirt down over her hips and swivelled in the mirror. 'What do you think?'

'Don't get me wrong,' I said, 'you look great, but...you don't look like my Mum.' I mean obviously she still had the same face, but that is where the similarity ended. My mother had never donned a short black skirt, or a red silk blouse. She'd certainly never worn a shade of lipstick that would match that blouse, or put on high, high heels.

'Does it matter how I dress?' she said.

'No, of course not.'

'Well then, tell Mother what the problem is.'

It was the most she'd sounded like the old Lorraine since she'd got there. 'There's no problem,' I said. 'This,' I waved my hand at her, 'new you is just going to take a little while to get used to.' I didn't want to tell her the truth because it was selfish and mean, and I knew if I voiced it out loud I would become less of a person.

What was my problem with the metamorphosis of my mother from a dull boring housewife to this vibrant glowing creature? Well the truth was *I* was used to being the rebel and the rule breaker, had taken a certain amount of pride in it. I had also taken comfort in the dullness of my mother, the one stable in my normally turmoil-filled life. If the person who was my contrast suddenly became like me then where did that leave me? Would I slowly morph into the old version of her? Would I become her contrast – the dull boring daughter, old before her time? The fact that the very thought of it terrified me meant it probably wouldn't happen, but deep inside, the fear niggled, and it lessened the pleasure I had at seeing my mother shine.

***

I awoke to the smell of bacon cooking and the noise of ceramic clacking. She may have been flitting around the kitchen in a skimpy camisole, rather than her full length nightie and slippers, but her urge to cook hadn't abated. She had taken charge of the catering situation a few days before when she'd looked in the fridge and hadn't found a single vegetable.

I had taken a leave day to finish an assignment that was due, but had put in such a good effort the night before that I only needed a few hours this morning to finish it. That meant I could go with Mum and Martine on a second-hand shopping spree. Martine had promised us there would be designer clothes galore at bargain basement prices. I could feel my pulse beating faster at the thought of it. It had been far too long between designer clothes for me.

We started at a small St Vincent's shop on the main drag, and to my delight some rich lady my size had dropped off a bundle of clothing the day before. Although her taste didn't exactly coincide with my own I managed to get a Gucci black velvet jacket and jeans at the bargain price of forty dollars.

Mum and I had a scuffle over a Louis Vuitton handbag, but I spotted the lining and realised it was a fake so I graciously let her win.

We were walking toward The Wayside Chapel – a community service centre that also housed a second-hand shop - and Mum and Martine were chatting about the club. I was concentrating on the feel of the sun on my face, enjoying the start of summer when I heard Mum screech.

A boy in a black hoodie had grabbed her handbag and was tug-o'-warring with her. As I watched, he reached out with his spare hand and shoved her to the ground. She still clung to her bag, screaming obscenities at him while Martine hit him over the head with her clutch. It would have looked hysterical to an onlooker, but the sight of him touching my Mother, hurting my Mother, filled me with fury. I let out a scream and launched myself at him, grabbing him around the waist and taking him to the ground.

'Get off me you crazy bitch,' he yelled, flipping over in my arms and getting his legs underneath him. He had Mum's bag tucked under his arm.

'I'm...not...crazy,' I said through my teeth as I held onto his pants.

He propelled himself upwards and away from me, slipping out of my grasp, and took off down the street. I jumped up and chased him, running as fast as I could in my Nine West sandals. I had managed to loosen his belt with my grappling and his pants were sliding down, limiting the length of his stride and allowing me to gain on him.

I caught him before he reached the next intersection, jumping onto his back and riding him down to the bitumen. I read him his rights as I snatched my handcuffs out of my bag (I felt safer when I had them with me) and snapped them onto one wrist. Pushing my knee into his lower spine I grabbed the other wrist and forced it behind his back till I had secured it as well. He was wiggling and screeching and by the time I had finished we had drawn quite a crowd.

I looked up to see Bob staring at me with his mouth wide open, a hot dog in one hand. 'Christ Chanel,' he said. Daniel was standing next to him, a small smile on his face.

'Bag snatcher,' I said, dragging the youth to his feet. I picked Mum's bag up off the ground and handed it to her. 'Do you want to take him in or should I?'

'You should do it,' Bob said.

I looked at him suspiciously. 'He's not undercover is he?'

'I doubt it,' Daniel said, 'he can't be eighteen.'

'Oh great, a minor,' I said in disgust. 'And you made me graze myself.' I looked down at the bleeding patches on my knees. That was going to hurt once the adrenaline wore off. 'Come with me,' I said to them, 'just in case he gets away.'

'From you?' Bob said shaking his head. 'Like to see him try.'

I arranged to meet Mum and Martine at a café and then propelled the youth up the road to the station.

'What's your name?' I said to the kid.

He declined to answer and I sighed.

'You may want to answer her,' Daniel said. 'You don't want to see her when she's angry.' He shot me a sideways look and smiled. It was the longest sentence I'd heard him say.

The kid grunted something.

'Pardon?' I said.

'It's Nick.'

We ran into Roger out the front of the station. 'What's this?' he asked.

'Chanel caught a bag snatcher,' Bob said.

'Well Chanel when you're finished with him can I have a word?'

'Sure,' I said, 'Bob's going to process him anyway seeing as how it's my day off.'

Bob shrugged and grasped Nick's elbow, leading him down the stairs and into the station. Daniel smiled at me over his shoulder and followed them in.

'Think you've got an admirer there,' Roger said.

'Who? Bob?'

'No, Daniel.'

'Don't be silly,' I said. 'We trained together, he's a friend.' The last thing I wanted was Roger holding off on any interest in me out of some misguided idea of there being something between Daniel and me. That's if he had any interest in me.

'Poor fellow,' he said, moving toward me. Then he looked around and leaned even closer. My breath caught in my throat and for one delicious second I thought he was going to kiss me.

But he didn't.

Instead he said, 'I went back to the last scene and guess what I found?'

'Really?' Even though I had known in my heart that it would be there, the knowledge that Roger had found it made my knees feel weak. *My God.* We finally had a lead on this monster.

'I spoke to your tobacconist and he's agreed to play.'

'Really? What did you say?'

'Let's just say it was in his best interest to help.' He winked at me.

I wasn't sure what that meant but I smiled and pretended I did. Did he have some dirt on the man that I didn't know about?

'So has he given you any names?'

'Not yet, but there can't be too many people smoking Coconut Hula Girl Cigars.'

'How do you know they're coconut?'

'They've got a pretty strong fragrance.'

Oh. He smelt them. I mentally kicked myself for not thinking of it. That was going to cut the list of suspects down dramatically.

'Thanks,' I said.

'What for?'

'For trusting me.'

'I'd be a fool to ignore any possible evidence. And besides,' he said, 'I never could say no to someone as cute as you.' He smiled and started to head back inside the station, giving me a fine view of his buttocks. No man should be allowed to wear such snuggly fitted trousers when their bottom was so fine. It was far too distracting.

'Chanel,' he said.

He was looking over his shoulder at me. *Oh great, totally sprung.*

'Here,' he said, a small smile on his face, 'my number just in case you think of something else.' He walked back and handed me his card, which I placed in my bag, too embarrassed to meet his eyes.

I walked back down the road to the café where Mum and Martine were waiting, my head awhirl with so many things. Part was replaying the chase and takedown of bag-snatching Nick, part was rejoicing in the fact that my hunch had paid off, but most of my brain was ridiculously preoccupied with the fact that Roger thought I was cute.

***

Mum was still asleep when I hopped up for work the next morning. She had been to Dazzle every night since she'd got here and I'd had to tell her about the serial killer to get her to promise to come home with Martine. She'd seemed a bit freaked out, which had pleased me. At least her good sense hadn't disappeared with her caterpillar eyebrows.

The front desk looked even more boring since having caught bag-snatching Nick. I wanted to be out there, making a difference. Not stuck signing in visitors and answering annoying phone calls.

The morning started with the annoying phone calls.

'Look sir,' I said after five minutes of listening to him give me reasons why he shouldn't be treated like everybody else. 'If your car's been impounded you're going to have to pay the fines before you can get it back. That's the whole point of it being impounded.'

He swore down the phone and hung up.

'Charming,' I said to no-one in particular.

'Chanel?' A small voice said.

I swung back to the front desk and saw Lizette standing just inside the door, one hand still holding it open as if she might bolt.

'Lizette,' I said, 'are you okay?'

Her eyes were red and puffy, but there was something else there as well. She glanced around and licked her lips, and I was reminded of a hunted animal.

I came out of the front room slowly, not wanting to startle her and held out my hand to her. 'It's all right,' I said, 'you can come in.'

She looked over her shoulder again and then scuttled towards me. She didn't take my hand but she let me lead her to a chair. She perched on its edge and folded her arms.

'I'm so sorry about Rosie,' I said.

'What do you care?'

'No-one deserves that,' I said.

'Not even a hooker?'

'No-one,' I repeated.

She stared at me for a second, her eyes hard, and then she seemed to wilt. Collapsing back into the chair she started to cry.

'She was my big sister,' she sobbed.

I let her cry herself out, unable to think of anything to say. Instead I put my arm around her and rocked her gently. She resisted for a second before leaning into me.

Eventually she stopped crying and said, 'We saw him.'

'Pardon,' I said.

She looked up at me and repeated herself. 'We saw him, the night he killed Leticia.'

Good God. Did she mean what I thought she did?

'The killer?' I confirmed.

She nodded her head.

'Would you know him again if you saw him?'

'I think so. We were on the other side of the road but he was under a light.'

'Did he see you?'

Her misery was palpable as she looked at me and I realised the stupidity of my question. Of course he did. That was why Rosie was dead and Lizette was here. She was scared she was next. She probably was.

'We can protect you,' I said.

'I don't know if you can,' she whispered.

'Yes, we can,' I said, 'but you have to let us.'

She stared into my eyes as if she were trying to decide if she could trust me. And then she nodded slightly.

'Okay,' I said. 'Let's get you inside and I'll go look for the detective in charge of the case.'

'I only want to speak to you.' Her body tensed up as if she were going to run and I put a hand gently on her shoulder.

'I'll be there,' I said, 'but you have to realise I don't have the power to help you.'

She looked uncertain, her eyes twitching towards the front door.

'But Detective Richardson does have that power,' I said.

She hopped up when I did and followed me into an interview room.

'Stay here,' I advised her. 'I'll get Roger.'

I ducked out the back, desperately hoping he was at his desk, but he wasn't.

'Daniel,' I said, spying him in the kitchenette, 'has Roger been in yet?'

'Haven't seen him,' he said. 'Hang on.' He walked over to the men's toilets and opened the door. 'Bob,' he yelled, 'have you seen Roger?'

I heard the toilet flush and a few seconds later Bob emerged. I found myself wondering if he'd stopped to wash his hands.

'Yep,' he said, looking over my head.

I swivelled and saw Roger coming through the door from the front area. 'Roger,' I said, 'you won't believe it; the sister of the last woman who was murdered is out the front. She says they saw the killer. That she can I.D. him.'

'Holy shit,' Bob said.

A look of something – triumph? – lit Roger's eyes and he grinned viciously. I found myself glad that I was on the same team.

'Wait,' I said as he turned. 'She wants me present.'

'Huh. Can you bring me a coffee then?'

I couldn't have taken a minute to make Roger's coffee but when I got back to the interview room Lizette was gone.

'Where is she?' he asked.

'She was right here.' I pointed at the empty chair. 'Maybe she's gone to the toilet.' But I knew better. Our major break in the case was gone. Run away on my watch. And I knew something else for sure. Once Ramy found out about it, my life was over.

***

Cocoa started tugging on the lead a few hundred metres before the park. Bruce was waiting. Or more accurately, Lancelot was. Cocoa and Lancelot's love affair was going from strength to strength. It was nice that he, at least, was getting some action.

'You look glum,' Bruce noted when I joined him on the love seat.

'Got my second warning today. One more and I'm out.'

'Why?'

'Lizette came in. Said she'd seen the killer. By the time I found Roger she was gone.'

'How is that your fault?'

'I should have stayed with her and gotten someone else to find Roger.'

'You couldn't have known she'd do a runner.'

'I know. But I should have been more careful.' In reality I didn't think it was worth a formal warning, but hey, I wasn't the Inspector in charge of the station. 'The bummer is that Roger walked right past her coming back from an interview.'

If only I'd stayed with her right now we might be bringing in the killer. As it was all we had was the Hula Girl butts and so far the tobacconist had come up chumps.

'You should come into the club,' he said, 'we'll cheer you up.'

'I've got to work early tomorrow.' I also wanted to look for Lizette once it got dark.

'We're rehearsing for a competition,' he said, 'your Mum's already there.'

That sentence left me with a heap of questions. I started with the most obvious. 'What competition?'

'It's a drag queen comp. The winners get to go to Las Vegas and perform.'

Wow, that was huge. 'Why is Mum there?'

'She's helping with the choreography.'

'Choreography?' What would Lorraine Smith of Hickery know about choreography? I hopped up from the bench. 'This I've got to see.'

Bruce kept up a happy chatter the whole way back to the club, for which I was grateful. I didn't feel like talking. Didn't feel like smiling. Didn't feel like doing anything but going home and eating a bucket of cookie cream commotion ice-cream. But I had to find Lizette. If she were working, it wouldn't be till after dark, so I may as well try to be sociable first.

Martine, Ronnie and the rest of the girls were up on stage dancing an unfamiliar routine. Ronnie pirouetted towards the front of the stage and picked up a waiting microphone. She sang as she swayed, waving her free arm in the air.

'She'll have sparklers,' Bruce told me as he handed me a drink. I thought about refusing it, but it was still a couple of hours till dark, and I didn't want to seem ungrateful.

All of a sudden Ronnie spun quickly to the side and peered back over her shoulder. The rest of the girls mirrored the move and it was apparent that Ronnie had gone the wrong way.

'No, no no.' Mum's voice rose over the music. The tune stopped and then Mum climbed onto the stage.

'I know,' Ronnie said, 'I went the wrong way.'

'And you got the words wrong,' Mum said. 'Here let me show you.'

Ronnie took Mum's spot and restarted the music at the beginning. I watched them dancing. Mum moved gracefully to the front of the stage and picked up the microphone. She looked into the distance, opened her mouth, and began to sing.

I thought I would cringe with the awkwardness of her voice. I thought I would be embarrassed to hear her croon. But the sweetness of her melody swept over me, carrying me away to a different time, a different place. It swelled with emotion, rich and smooth, bringing tears to my eyes.

I hadn't known she could sing. Hadn't known she could dance. But I watched her prance and jive and swirl around the stage, and at the end of the song I was left wanting more. I was also left with about a million questions. When had she learnt to dance? How come she could choreograph such a complex routine? If she could sing like *that* what had she been doing living in Hickery?

My questions had to wait till they had finished rehearsing and she made her way, glistening with sweat, to the bar.

'Oh hello,' she said, spying me sitting on one of the stools. Cocoa and Lancelot had curled up at my feet and were asleep, their bodies a blended bundle of black.

I looked at her while I tried to think of what to say. Part of me wished I could go back to the way it had been. This version of my mother, while more fun, was someone I didn't know. I wanted to go back to a time when she had been boring and predictable and, if I were brutally honest with myself, when her main priority had been me. When *I* had been the blazing star in her sky and she had lived vicariously through me. But I felt like it had all been a lie; a lie that took away from what I was by making a mockery of my past.

And so I did the only thing I could think of. I grabbed Cocoa and I went home to my tub of cookie cream commotion ice-cream.

***

I was half way through the container when I heard her key in the lock. She stood in the doorway, watching me on the lounge. I could see Martine hovering behind her in the hall.

'That's what you're eating for dinner?' she said.

'My mother was off singing and dancing.' It was rude and not fair and I knew it even before the words came out of my mouth. But I said them anyway. It had been a pretty rough day as they go, but it was still no excuse.

'You survived before I got here,' she said, dropping her bag on the kitchen bench.

I sighed and put the lid back on the container. 'Do you want some?' I asked. She recognised it for the peace offering that it was. I normally don't share my ice-cream.

'Sure,' she said. She grabbed two spoons and she and Martine took turns eating the rest of the tub.

When they had finished she turned to me and said. 'I used to be a showgirl in Las Vegas.'

'A showgirl? In Las Vegas?' I slumped back into the couch, my mouth opening and closing with no noise coming out. To be truthful I had no idea how to comprehend the news.

'I met Harry while I was over there. He was on holidays.'

'Harry?' Martine asked.

'Chanel's father. I found out I was pregnant after he left, so I followed him back to Australia.'

'Las Vegas?' I said again.

'What's wrong with Las Vegas?'

'Nothing. I think I may be in shock.' I guess this was the sort of stuff I would have heard about at family gatherings, if we had any family. Mum's parents had died before I was born, and she had been an only child. I knew nothing of my Dad's side.

How long were you there for?' Martine asked.

'Three years. I was young and stupid. I should have stayed. But I thought Harry was the be-all-

and-end-all. Turned out he didn't feel the same way about me.'

Poor Mum. She'd had her heart broken and then sacrificed everything to raise me by herself. I had no right to give her a hard time about anything. 'I'm sorry,' I said, holding her hand. 'I know I'm being awful. It's just a lot to take in.'

'But you'll take it in?'

'Eventually. Until then I'll pretend I have.' I looked out the window and noticed that the sun had finally gone down. 'Shit,' I said, standing. 'I have to find Lizette.'

'Why?' Martine asked.

I filled them in on the day's activities.

'You're not going out by yourself,' Mum said, standing up.

'We're coming with you,' Martine added.

I made a few noises about it being too dangerous but the truth was I welcomed their company; safety in numbers and all that.

'All right,' I said after a decent amount of time, 'but we're wearing sensible shoes.' If I had to watch Mum and Martine running shrieking from the killer in skyscraper high heels there was a chance I'd get caught when I fell over laughing.

We had no luck finding Lizette on the main streets of the Cross. Eventually we ran into Bianca who gave us directions to the apartment Lizette had shared with Rosie. It was in the seedier part of town, where the street lights were spaced far apart and the shadows were long and spooky. Her apartment backed onto a lane, and after a few minutes of knocking on her door and calling her name we went around the back to see if there was any movement through the windows.

The lane was dark and scary, as most lanes in King's Cross tended to be. The place was the perfect setting for a horror movie.

'She just *had* to live in the last building, didn't she,' I muttered to Mum and Martine.

I was glad they were with me; there was no way I would have had the courage to come down here by myself. As it was I was at the pee-my-pants end of terror.

Finally we made it to her building and I stared up at it while I tried to work out which apartment was hers. 'It's this one,' I said, moving to stand under a darkened window.

I wasn't looking where I was going, so I guess I shouldn't have been surprised when my foot caught in a pile of rubbish. My momentum carried me forwards and without the use of my left foot I stumbled and fell, crashing through the nest of newspaper and onto something soft. My first thought, as I floundered around trying to get my feet back underneath me, was that I had landed on a homeless person.

I could feel hands, Martine's by the size, helping me up. Once I was standing I looked down into the mess.

Blood rushed to my head, my vision tunnelled, and for a minute everything became very strange.

Reality turned into snapshots of time, each one holding my attention perfectly until the next one intruded.

Lizette, curled into a foetal position.

Round, red welts cover her arms.

An open pink bag, its contents spewed onto the ground.

A ragged gash in her neck.

Someone is screaming.

Martine bent at the waist, liquid splattering the pavement.

Something red smeared on my shirt.

Mum's mouth moving in slow motion.

My hands, coated with a wet red liquid.

Mum, shaking my shoulders.

Oh my God, it's blood. It's her blood.

She's dead, she's dead, she's dead.

The sting of a hand contacted with my cheek. My head snapped to the side and the screaming stopped as I drew in a sharp breath. And then my vision spiralled outwards and normality returned.

Mum stood in front of me, her hand raised to strike again.

'I'm okay,' I said, panting. Tears streamed down my face. I hadn't realised I was crying. But then I hadn't realised I'd been screaming either.

Poor Lizette: so young and vulnerable, so very, very dead.

I resisted the urge to start wailing again and instead dug around inside my bag, emerging with a small rectangle of cardboard. I punched the numbers on the card into my phone. It rang three times before it was answered.

'Yes?' Roger said. I could hear water in the background? Was he showering? Was he at this very moment naked? The thought would have distracted me if the nature of my call had not been so serious.

'Lizette is dead.' I sniffled and wiped my nose on my shirt.

'Chanel?'

'The one and only.'

'Where are you?'

I gave him the address, hoping he would be there fast. I waited for him on the corner of the lane trying not to think about three things.

She was still warm. She hadn't been dead very long. The killer was near.

Roger turned up as quickly as I had hoped, another car with a forensic team not that far behind.

'Did you touch the crime scene?' he said.

'I fell on her.' I shuddered at the memory. 'She was hidden under garbage.'

'What were you doing here?' His voice was exasperated.

'I wanted to talk to her.' A tear trailed down my cheek. I had failed badly.

He reached out and brushed it away and then pulled me into an embrace. When he let me go – far too quickly I might add – he shook his head. 'You're like some sort of danger magnet,' he said. 'I think I should keep you closer.' And then he walked off to examine the body.

Martine and Mum were huddled by the corner. Martine's make-up was a mess. Mascara trailed down her face, lipstick smudged her cheeks and hands. Mum on the other hand seemed quite composed. I guess it helped that she hadn't known Lizette, but even then, I had vomited at my first body.

We were all interviewed before we were allowed to go, so it was near midnight before we were safely home. 'You all right,' I asked Mum. I was worried she might be in shock.

'You see a lot of dead bodies when you live in Las Vegas,' she said, shrugging a shoulder. 'I know it was a long time ago, but that sort of thing, well... it stains your soul.'

I knew what she meant. My horror tonight hadn't just been about a corpse. This had been personal. Lizette had made her own choices, but I had let her down.

Killer one, Chanel none. It was time to try and even the score.

Chapter Ten

Just When I Thought Things Couldn't Get Worse...

I wasn't surprised when Roger came in late the next day. They must have been there till the wee hours of the morning. I *was* surprised when Ramy called me into his office and took me off desk duty.

Roger was waiting for me when I re-emerged, dizzy with the relief of not having been given my last formal warning. 'Howdy partner,' he said.

'You look like shit,' I told him. It wasn't true at all. He may have looked tired and unshaven but he still looked sexy as hell. I peered closer, admiring the view. 'Is that a black eye?'

'You should see the other guy.' He smiled and winked. 'Come on Bun, let's get out of here.'

'Me with you?'

'I told you last night, I'm going to keep you closer.'

Dear God. I had trouble framing a coherent sentence when he was close enough to smell his aftershave. I didn't know how I was going to go if I was permanently on the beat with him.

'Did you speak to Ramy?' I had assumed the cessation of my desk duty punishment was to allow some other sucker the position.

'That. And Bob's being punished for his slovenly appearance.'

'He does get a lot of tomato sauce on his shirt.'

'Yesterday a pensioner with a dicky heart thought it was blood and they had to call an ambulance.'

I was almost sure he was joking, but in this game the weirdest things happened.

As Roger and I were heading towards the front door we saw Daniel running down the stairs. 'Fire!' he yelled as he opened the door.

'Where?' Roger asked.

'Up the road at the shops. I think it's the tobacconist.'

Roger turned to look at me. I was pretty sure the horror on his face mirrored my own.

I could smell the smoke as soon as we left the building, taste the sootiness in the air. Roger was much faster than I was and he left me far behind as we raced towards the shop.

Pillars of flame were already licking up the second storey of the building; the tobacconist was a ball of fire. Bystanders were gathered on the other side of the road watching the disaster unfold.

'Did anybody come out?' Roger yelled at them.

'They didn't have time,' a man with a Zimmer frame said. 'There was an explosion about five minutes ago.'

Roger raced to the side lane, where a small door exited the shop. I watched him touch the back of his hand to the handle and then he grasped it and pulled. I'm still not sure if there was a second detonation, or if the influx of oxygen to the previously sealed site fed the flames to a ferocious new intensity, but as Roger opened the door a wall of flames shot out through the opening. They coalesced on him, lovingly licking his body.

'No,' I screamed as I ran towards him.

He dropped to the ground and rolled, trying to extinguish the fire which burned on the front of his uniform. I leapt on top of him, smothering them with my body, but the damage was already done.

'Ah shit,' he said as he looked down. The fire had burnt through his shirt in multiple places, and the red raw flesh of his stomach was visible. He sniffed at it. 'Smells like chicken.'

'That's the worst joke I've ever heard,' I said, climbing carefully off him.

I looked down at his gut. Most of it was blistered but in some areas the blisters had been torn by his attempts to stop the flames. All in all it didn't look too bad. But that's the thing about burns - they look their best when they're fresh.

'That's got to hurt,' I said. 'I mean I'm hurting just looking at it.'

'Actually,' he said, pushing my arm back, 'you're burnt too.'

I looked down at my arm. There was a burn the size of a small egg on the front of my forearm. It was nothing compared to Roger's though, so I bit my tongue and tried to ignore the pain.

His face convulsed and he lay back on the pavement breathing rapidly. I could hear the fire brigade's approach and I was praying there was an ambulance with it. I wanted to stay with him, but I knew he would be better served by my action than my company. I staggered up off the ground and down to the street. The ambulance was visible behind the fire truck so I waved them down and brought them up to Roger. Crouching down beside him I took his hand in mine.

'That looks pretty nasty mate,' Steve, the ambulance officer said. He handed Roger a green plastic pipe. Roger put one end in his mouth and puffed on it and then lay back with a grin on his face.

'What is that?' I said to Steve.

'The green whistle.'

I stared at him blankly.

'Methoxyflurane. Penthrox.'

I still had no idea what he was talking about, but by the look on Roger's face I was guessing it was some good shit.

'Bun,' Roger said, staring up at me. He took another puff of the green whistle and giggled. 'Cute bunny bun.'

I didn't know what it was but I had to get me some of it.

'Bunny bun, will you go out with me?'

'Will he remember this tomorrow?' I asked Steve.

'Probably not.'

'Bunny got burnt too,' Roger said. He reached up and undid the top button on my work blouse and pulled it open. Damn the burns and the audience, I was wishing we were alone and all our skin was intact.

'Actually it's on my arm,' I said, holding it up for Steve to see, 'and it's nothing.'

I was desperately hoping he'd hand me one of those green thingies as well, but he looked at it and said, 'It's going to hurt, (like I didn't know that) we'll take you to the hospital and get it looked at.'

Given the options of going back to work and possibly being put back on the front counter versus a free ride in an ambulance, I was going to take the ambulance ride every time. I let them bundle me into the back with Roger who clutched me with one hand and the green train with the other.

'Here,' Roger said, handing me the whistle.

I thought about refusing it. But hey, my arm was really stinging. 'Thanks,' I said, taking a puff.

Man that stuff was awesome. I handed it to Roger and sank back against the other stretcher.

'I meant what I said Bun.' Roger seemed to be having a lucid moment but I was in lala land. 'Chanel.' He shook my hand.

'Yeah.' I could still feel the pain in my arm but it was faint and distant, as if it belonged to a Chanel in a different time space continuum.

'I meant it when I asked you out.'

'Roger,' I said, 'you shouldn't be thinking about things like that. You need to concentrate on getting better.'

'Promise me you'll go out with me and that will help me focus on getting better.'

He looked so handsome, so vulnerable, lying on that stretcher. A pale sheen of sweat covered his face. His blue eyes were still bright but as I watched they creased with the effort of controlling the pain.

'All right,' I said, 'I'll go out on a date with you. Now suck that damned whistle.'

'You're even cuter when you're worried,' he said, smiling. He lay his head back down and lifted the green whistle to his lips.

It didn't take long to get to the hospital. They wheeled us into the emergency ward and the doctors took Roger straight through into the treatment area. I was handed over to a nurse who gave me some painkillers and then dressed my burn.

'Can you tell me how Detective Richardson is?' I asked her when she had finished.

'Was that the officer you came in with?'

I nodded my head while I examined my bandage.

'Wait here,' she told me, 'I'll go see.'

The look on her face was grave when she came back. 'He's got third degree burns and is going to need skin grafts.'

Skin grafts? That didn't sound like fun.

I couldn't think of a reason to hang around any longer, except maybe to check out the doctors - and that didn't seem right given the situation Roger was in - so I managed to get Steve to give me a lift back to the station.

Ramy sent me home for the day on sick leave but before I left I found out from Bob that a body had been retrieved from the fire. It was so badly burnt they would need forensics to identify it but my money was on it being the shop owner.

A paid day off is on my list of top ten favourite things. Unfortunately the pain from my burn made it impossible to do anything enjoyable. I took some more painkillers and lay on my bed with Cocoa while Mum fussed around me. She headed off to Dazzle in the early afternoon to start rehearsals for the competition which left me with far too much thinking time. My thoughts went round and round.

The old man had said there was an explosion. Had it been an accident? Was it possible the fire had been coincidental and nothing to do with our investigation?

And then I remembered something. Last night there had been one main difference at the crime scene. Lizette's arms had been covered with burns from something the size of a cigarette. Or a Hula Girl Cigar. Why would the killer have done that this time?

And then the next morning the very shop that sold those cigars was burnt to the ground, possibly with the person who had the information we needed in it.

Was it possible the tobacconist had questioned the killer? Had the killer become suspicious? Had he gone back to the other sites and realised that the butts he left were gone?

A cold sweat broke out on my body and suddenly I knew for sure. He had known when he'd killed Lizette we were on to him. He had eliminated the last witness and then gone after our informant. He was clever and deadly and he had to be stopped. I just hoped we had the information we needed to do it, and I wouldn't know that till I could talk to Roger.

***

Talking to Roger was harder than it sounded. I mean it's impossible to have a two way conversation with someone who is in a coma. I had freaked out when the nurse had told me, until she had explained it was a medically induced coma.

'The pain would be too much for him to bear, deary. It's the kindest way for him to heal.'

I mean I really wanted Roger to heal, the faster the better – it was dead boring at work without him, but I also wanted to know if the poor tobacconist (may he rest in peace) had given him any names. I was guessing the DNA results would be back by now and it was possible we were holding all the cards where the killer was involved.

He was in a coma for a week, and then the next couple of times I visited he was asleep. I was so tempted to wake him, but even asleep his face held the shadow of pain, and I didn't want to wake him to that.

It was almost two weeks after the accident that I finally got to talk to Roger. He was sitting up in bed, reading the newspaper when I arrived one afternoon after work.

'Bun.' He sounded delighted to see me. I wondered if he remembered asking me out on a date.

'I would have brought flowers but I'm only a Probationary Constable so I can't afford any,' I said.

He smiled and patted the side of the bed. If the expression on his face was anything to go by, even that small movement had been painful.

I perched there precariously, trying to get comfortable without jostling him. 'How's it going?' I said, nodding my head towards his stomach.

'I was lucky, it was only medium rare.' He moved a leg and winced. 'Skin graft,' he said, pointing at it.

'They took it from there?'

He nodded his head, watching my face with a smile. 'Go on.'

'What?' I said.

'You know you want to ask.'

'I don't know what you're talking about,' I said.

'You want to know what colour the hair on my legs is.'

I could feel myself blushing profusely. 'I do not. But since you obviously want to talk about it will it be a different colour?'

He laughed. 'You'll have to wait and see.'

Christ. If my face got any brighter you'd be able to put me on a Christmas tree. I was having trouble breathing being that close to him. He wasn't wearing any aftershave but he still smelt earthy and salty and...manly. Did he taste salty? I had a sudden urge to lick his neck.

'Did the results come back?' I said.

'Yes and I'm pregnant.'

'Be serious,' I said.

'I am serious and don't call me Shirley.'

I looked at the intravenous tube coming out of his arm. 'What are they giving you?'

'Pethadeine.'

'I'm not going to get a sensible sentence out of you am I?'

'Probably not.'

I sighed. 'Shall I come back tomorrow?'

'Yes and don't spare the horses.'

***

Mum was packing her bags when I got home. She looked up when I came through the door. 'I'm moving out.'

'Is it me?' I probably hadn't been the best flatmate over the last couple of weeks.

'No silly. Another apartment came up in the building. We're going to be neighbours.'

'Mum, how are you going to afford the rent?'

'Well with the rent I'm getting for the house in Hickery and with what Bruce is paying me...'

'Whoa, back up. Bruce is paying you?'

'His wardrobe lady left.'

'So you'll be making the costumes?'

'I'll be handling the show side of things so Bruce can concentrate on the marketing.' She wrestled the zipper on her last bag shut and stood up.

'When do you leave?'

The words were just out of my mouth when there was a knock on my door.

'Oh that'll be the moving man,' she said.

'Why do you need a moving man?'

She flitted over to the front door and opened it. Joe, the landlord, was standing in the door, shirt half unbuttoned, gold chains visible. He had made a special effort with his dark hair, slicking it up and back. My fingers itched to style it properly.

He had a bunch of flowers in one hand which he handed to Mum and said, 'I've come to welcome you to your new home.'

'I didn't get any flowers,' I complained.

'They're lovely,' Mum said, ignoring me. She buried her face in them and giggled.

I sighed as I picked up a couple of her bags. Mum grabbed the others, but Joe relieved her of hers before she made it out the front door. Joe and I lugged her stuff up another floor to her apartment, while Mum flirted unabashedly. I had to admit she was good. If my performance whenever Roger was around was anything to go by I should have been taking notes.

Giggle, bat your eyelids, look at said conquest through those eyelashes and giggle again. For some reason I didn't think I'd pull that off with Roger; especially not while he was on pethadeine.

I could tell that Joe was going to hang around for a while so I went back downstairs, grabbed Cocoa's lead and took him to the park.

Bruce was waiting.

'How's the case going?' he asked.

'So not broken,' I said. 'Roger's either asleep or on drugs. I can't get a serious word out of him. How's Bianca going?' Since Lizette had been killed most of the hookers had decided it was time to take some annual leave. Bianca had decided it was time to give it up for good and had taken a barmaid position.

'Surprisingly good. She's efficient and in her words, she don't take shit from nobody.'

'The perfect barmaid.'

'She's been asking when you're coming in again. Seems to have taken quite a shine to you.'

'Tell her I'm on days off on Thursday. I'll come that night.'

'You should come early and check out the new routine your Mammy's teaching the girls.'

'What's it like?'

'That would ruin the surprise.'

Great. Another surprise involving my Mum. I wasn't sure how many more of them I could take.

***

Roger was looking more lucid when I got there the next afternoon.

'No pethadeine?' I said, viewing his arm.

'They took the drip out this morning. Shame,' he said.

'You seemed to be enjoying yourself.'

He grinned. 'Apart from the pain and suffering and all that, I've been having a grand old time. Best holiday I've had in years.'

'Lucky you,' I said, taking a seat on the end of his bed. 'We need to talk.'

'The case?'

'Yep.'

'You heard they found evidence of arson?'

I nodded my head. 'And that the tobacconist died?'

'Poor bastard,' he said.

'Did you get any names from him?'

'He gave me two,' he said. 'But neither of them matches the DNA on the butts.'

'They were all the same?'

He nodded. 'All smoked by the same person, but they're not currently on the register.'

'So that's that,' I said, disappointment flooding through me.

He ran a hand through his hair and sighed. 'We have the DNA.'

'It's weird,' I said, 'there haven't been any more killings since the fire.'

He looked thoughtful for a few moments before saying, 'We drove him underground.'

'Drove who where?'

'The killer. He knew we were on to him, so he destroyed the trail and vanished. Reminds me of a case we had in London.'

'You caught a serial killer in London?'

'No. We never caught him.' He scratched the stubble on his face. 'Well not while I was there. They may have caught him since.'

'What happened?'

'Pretty similar details, someone targeting prostitutes. Every time we got close to the bastard he disappeared, only to reactivate later in another part of London.' He looked off into the distance, his blue eyes pensive. 'We chased him for years.'

'God I hope we get this one soon,' I said. I looked at my watch. I was meant to be meeting Bruce in half an hour. 'Got to go,' I said, standing up.

He grabbed my hand and ran his thumb over my palm. I could feel little shivers of pleasure expanding all the way down to my fingertips. 'Thanks for visiting,' he said.

I didn't know if I was ever going to get used to his face. It wasn't classically handsome, but it was the most attractive face I knew. When he smiled it was like summer and ice-cream and chocolate all mixed up together. Nobody else had ever had that effect on me.

No problem,' I mumbled. I was enjoying the feeling of him stroking my hand *way* too much. I detached before it would look too sad and headed towards the corridor.

'Hey Bun,' he called out.

I paused and looked over my shoulder.

'I haven't forgotten,' he said. And then he closed his eyes.

***

The stage was different when I got to Dazzle that Thursday. There were long silver poles extending from the floor to the ceiling. Mum stood in front of one talking to the girls. As I watched she grasped it with her hands and flipped upside down. She did the splits with one leg either side of the pole before flicking back to the ground.

'That's called the Hello Boys,' Bruce informed me as he handed me a cocktail.

A mob of drag queens doing a Hello Boys? *Good Grief.*

'This audience is going to get far more than they've bargained for.' I looked at the drink. 'I could need something stronger.'

He grinned and whisked it off, returning it a few moments later. I took a sip and nodded. It might almost be strong enough to erase the memory of my mother pole dancing.

'Hey superwoman,' Bianca said.

'I'm no superwoman,' I said, smiling at her. She had toned her outfit down just a little; and a mean *just* a little. The black and pink Dazzle T-shirt looked like it had shrunk in the wash, showing an expanse of smooth chocolate belly before the obligatory black pants began. There was a pink crystal hanging from the piercing at her navel.

She placed her index finger on her chin and peered at me. 'You're right,' she said. 'I'm getting more of a cat woman vibe from you. You know, with the slashed black pants and the cute little mask. You'd look sexy as hell in that outfit.'

'I'll keep that in mind next time I have a date.' That, of course, made me think of Roger. I took another long sip of my cocktail.

'You got boy problems?'

'I've got *man* problems,' I said. I could feel the alcohol searing through my arteries. It felt really good.

'Is it that blonde cop with the sexy accent and the biteable arse?'

'That's the one.'

She took a seat next to me at the bar. 'I bet he's a fine ride.'

'*Bianca*,' I said, swatting at her with one hand.

'You can tell me,' she said. 'Sex is…was my business.'

'How's this working out for you?' I asked.

'It's nice to have the regular income,' she said.

I wasn't sure if I was mature enough to have this conversation. The alcohol in my brain thought differently.

'Surely there have to be some other advantages,' I said.

'Well, it will be nice not to be cold in winter,' she said. 'It's a long time between clients in winter.'

'What about…you know,' I said.

'I know what?'

'Well isn't it nice not to have to sleep with strangers?' I can't believe I actually said it. Part of me was gasping at my audacity but the other part was totally into this conversation.

'It wasn't all bad,' she said. 'I kind of got my regulars you know. And if you don't think about it, when you're with a regular, you could be on a date. Except you get paid at the end, and you don't have to cook them dinner every night.' She grinned at me.

'Geez, when you put it like that it's better than having a boyfriend.'

'Nah, there's some nasty shit too.'

Even the interested part of me agreed that it didn't want to know the details of the nasty shit.

'Will you go back to it,' I said, 'once we've caught the killer?'

She looked thoughtful as she pulled on the end of her thick black ponytail. 'I don't think so,' she said. 'I want different things now. When I started turning tricks it was the easiest way to make money. I'd like to study you know.' She tugged some more on her hair. 'And I'd like to get married and have a family one day.'

The girls up on stage were in the process of clambering up the pole. I could hear Mum's voice counting in time with her clapping. 'And one and two and three ... no no Bernadette. It's climb and climb and dying swan.'

'Dying swan?' I mouthed at Bianca.

She hopped off the stool. 'A mob of drag queens performing a dying swan on a pole? One less thing I have to see before I die.'

Bruce flicked her on the bottom with a tea towel. 'Get back to work,' he said.

She winked at me and sashayed off to the kitchen.

Mum called a break and came over to join me at the bar. I hadn't seen much of her since she'd moved out, and even though I wouldn't admit it to her, I'd missed her.

'Pole dancing?' I said, taking another pull on my straw.

'It's a bit like falling off a bike,' she said.

'Don't you mean like riding a bike?'

'No, like falling off one; it hurts every time you do it.' She brayed out a laugh and hit me on the shoulder. Unfortunately she chose the arm holding my drink.

I mopped it off the front of my dress with a serviette and then said, 'How's Joe going?'

'He's fun,' she said, smiling widely.

'I so don't want to know what that means.' Sadly, I was far more comfortable talking to Bianca about her profession than I was talking to my Mum about her sex life. 'You changed your hair colour,' I said.

'Don't you like it?'

'It's red. What's not to like. I just want to know why I didn't do it.'

'Well to be honest,' she said, 'I didn't think you wanted to do that sort of thing any more.'

'Why ever not?'

'Well you're an important police officer now.'

I snorted some cocktail out of my mouth. 'Important police officer?' I said. 'I'm a bee's dick from having to go back to hairdressing.'

It was only a matter of time really. If I could drum up two formal warnings in my first six weeks without even trying, I was never going to make it to a year. I had been pinning my hopes on helping catch the Cross killer. I thought if that happened then maybe Ramy would forget about my prior convictions. Those hopes had been destroyed along with the tobacconist's shop.

'When's the competition?' I asked her.

'Next Friday night. Can you come?'

I counted forward on my fingers. I'd be on days off. 'Wouldn't miss it for the world,' I said.

***

Helping a band of drag queens train for a pole dancing routine was not something I would have normally signed up for, but Mum had turned on the I-sacrificed-everything-to-raise-you charm and guilted me into it. The old Lorraine would never have done that, but this was the new Lorraine we were talking about, so all bets were off.

Pole dancing was both easier and harder than I had expected. The girls were starting to master their routine, which was good as it was only a couple of days till the competition.

I was having a water break when I realised I had missed a call from Roger.

'Bun,' he said, when I called him back. 'Good news, they're releasing me.'

'Outstayed your welcome?'

'They were worried the nurses were becoming too attached.'

That was probably true. I'd witnessed at least two different nurses flirting and giggling helplessly when they were in his room.

'Anyway I was wondering if you could give me a lift home,' he said. 'Unless you're doing something important.'

I looked over at the stage where Ronnie was stuck upside down on a pole. She clung to it with her arms and legs while Mum tried to talk her down. 'Not anymore,' I said, picking up my handbag.

'I'll wait for you outside the entrance,' he said.

'Sure you don't want me to come up and help you?'

'I'll be right.'

'Give me half an hour,' I said, calculating how long it would take me to walk home and get the car.

It was dark in the car park so I didn't see the mess on the windscreen till I was seated in the car. Blood was smeared all over the glass, as if someone had used a bloody cloth to wash it. Bits of dark fur clung to the blood and a black shape lay on the bonnet. Dead. Ice walked down my spine and I couldn't move. I stared at the shape, fear and anguish bubbling up inside.

'Cocoa, oh no Cocoa,' I moaned.

The tears came with my voice, sobs ripping through me.

I clambered out of the car, clutching at the door as my legs refused to take my weight. I dragged myself around the door to the bonnet and pulled the shape towards me, crushing it to my chest. And then I realised… it wasn't Cocoa at all.

Some sick bastard had killed a huge black rabbit and emptied it out on my car. I turned and vomited next to the driver's side door. And then I cried some more.

When I had finished I replaced the rabbit and pulled out the torch I kept in my handbag. Who would have thought there would be so much blood in one rabbit?

I barely had it together again when I saw the letters drawn in the mess on the windscreen.

YOU'RE NEXT BITCH.

I'd have thought that would undo me, but instead I went into some form of shock. My knees stopped shaking, my stomach stopped churning and I pulled my phone out and rang Roger.

'My car just became a crime scene,' I said, when he answered.

'Have you had an accident?'

'No. Some sicko killed a rabbit and left it on my car with a message for me.' Someone who knew I had a black dog, someone who knew where I lived, someone who wanted to scare me. I could feel my knees starting to shake again so I pushed those thoughts to the back of my mind.

'I'm sorry,' I said, 'I can't come and get you.'

'Jesus,' he said. 'I'll get a cab. Where do you live?'

It seemed almost natural for him to come to my aid. I gave him the address and then rang work. Jake, a constable on the opposite shifts to me, was on the front desk. I managed to restrain myself from asking what he'd done to deserve that and instead told him about the car.

Roger arrived before they did. He was walking slowly and carefully and his face creased every now and then with pain. 'Jesus,' he said again, staring at the car.

'Do you think?' I said.

'That it's him?'

'Yeah.'

'Who else have you pissed off?'

'No-one that I know of. I've been on the front desk most of the time.'

We both stared at the bonnet and as the full import of the words sunk in I started to shake. How had he found out about me? The tobacconist must have told him, it was the only way. Then he'd waited outside the station for me and followed me home. He'd seen me out walking Cocoa. What else had he seen? Who else was in danger?

'Mum,' I said.

'I must admit, that was not the word I was expecting.'

'Mum could be in danger,' I said. 'I have to ring her.'

Nathan and Mark turned up while I was dialling Mum's number. I could hear Roger filling them in.

I left a message for her and rang Bruce. He picked up just when I was starting to think I would get his voicemail as well. I told him what had happened and he promised to make sure that everybody went home in groups of at least three. Feeling slightly better I hung up and went back to the grisly mess on my car.

They were taking photos of it and I could see they were going to be a while.

'Do you mind if I go check on Cocoa?' I said to Roger. 'And I wouldn't mind changing.' Once again I had blood all over the front of my shirt. It seemed to be becoming a habit.

'I'll come with you,' Roger said, 'just in case...'

Just in case the killer was waiting for me in my apartment. Was this what my life was going to be like from now on? Always looking over my shoulder, always expecting the worst? All of a sudden life as a hairdresser didn't seem like such a bad thing.

We paused outside my door. 'Do you have your gun?' Roger asked.

'Is that a trick question?' My gun was exactly where it was meant to be. At work, secure in my locker.

'Well I don't have mine either.'

'And you're in no state to fight.'

'We make a great couple.'

'The two stooges. Luckily' I said, 'Cocoa's had attack training.' I placed the key in the lock and turned it slowly. I wasn't sure if I made any noise or not because I couldn't hear anything over the thudding of my heart.

Cocoa launched himself at me as I opened the door and I hugged him to my chest. I buried my face in his fur and then remembered I was meant to be checking to make sure there was no killer hiding in my apartment.

From Cocoa's reaction when I got home I was pretty sure no-one was there. If there were, I would have expected him to show some sign of it. Bark or point a paw at the hiding place.

Yeah right.

All the killer would have had to do to win Cocoa's undying love was to give him a treat on arrival.

I set Cocoa down and progressed slowly into the apartment, Roger beside me. I grabbed a knife from the kitchen and then put it back and grabbed a rolling pin.

'Less messy,' I whispered. The truth was while I didn't mind the thought of hitting someone over the head with a rolling pin I couldn't fathom the thought of sticking a knife into them. I mean that would really hurt.

I have screwed up ethics, I know.

The advantage of living in such a small apartment was that there were fewer places to search. Once we'd checked the four corners of the living area and the bathroom we were pretty much done. The mezzanine floor that housed the bed was totally visible from the lounge.

Cocoa was making friends with Roger, snuffling around his legs and whining.

'That was a joke about the attack training wasn't it? Roger asked.

'Nope.'

'So if I said attack he would?' He watched Cocoa warily.

'Yes, but you have to say it like you mean it.'

'Attack,' he said, in a loud voice.

Cocoa snarled and leapt at Roger, attempting to fasten his teeth onto his forearm.

'Release,' I shrieked in horror.

He stopped his attack and sat, wagging his tail and waiting for a treat.

'Jesus,' Roger said, 'I thought you were joking.'

'Are you okay?' I grabbed his arm to inspect it. An electric shock raced up my fingers and all of a sudden I wanted to touch his skin in a totally different way.

'He didn't hurt me,' he said softly.

I let go of his arm before I could make a fool of myself. 'I need to change,' I said, backing away from him.

I grabbed a clean shirt from my wardrobe and hurried into the bathroom. The blood had seeped through the cotton of my top and onto my bra and stomach. Sighing I went back to grab a new bra.

'I need a shower,' I told Roger. He was sitting on the couch with Cocoa jammed against his thigh, idly stroking Cocoa's coat. The sight of that didn't help me at all. It was possible, apart from an inability to wash his own coffee cup, that Roger was the perfect man; I just didn't know what to do about it.

The shower water felt great against my body as I soaped off the blood. Of course half way through I realised that Roger was on the other side of the very thin wall and all of a sudden a cold shower would have been more beneficial. I was drying myself off when he knocked on the door.

I wrapped myself in a bathrobe and opened the door wide enough to speak. His face was at the door opening and suddenly I found myself so close I could feel his breath on my cheek. I froze. A few seconds passed, neither of us moving and then he lifted a hand and touched my face. His eyes softened as he stared into mine, and then he pulled the door open, gathered me to him and kissed me.

It started as a slow kiss; our lips stroking tantalisingly over each other's. My mind was whirling, unable to believe that it was getting what it had craved. I parted my lips, tasting him with my tongue and he tightened his hold on me, moving one hand from my face, down the robe to the small of my back.

The kiss deepened. Sensation left all parts of my body except those he touched; my lips, my face, the length of my body that he pressed against. All I could feel, all I could smell, all I could hear, was him. He turned me, pressing my back against the wall, leaning into me as he ravished my lips and my mind.

The kiss quickened. His other hand trailed softly down my neck, along my collar bone and then it stopped at the edge of my robe. I pressed against him, eager for him to feel more of my skin, more of me. Finally, his hand slipped under the edge of my robe and trailed down the bare skin of my belly and then back up to the curve of my breast.

I moaned against his mouth and felt him stiffening in response to the feel of me. His hand caressed the skin of my breast, brushing lightly over my nipple. I pulled up his shirt and ran my hands down his chest, pausing at the feel of his bandages.

'It's okay,' he whispered, moving his mouth from my lips to my neck.

The feel of him on me, touching me, kissing me, it was more intense that I could have imagined. I was gone. I was his to do whatever he wanted to, for however long he wanted to. And I was hoping he was going to take a very long time.

Just as his other hand was pushing my robe out of the way I heard a knock at the door. He started to pull away.

'Ignore it,' I said urgently, pulling his mouth back to mine.

He did, for a second but then he pulled away again and smiled. 'I was going to tell you, before you distracted me, that the boys were on their way up to interview you.'

I pouted and started to cover myself but he put a hand out to stop me. Looking down at my half-open robe he shook his head. 'I should arrest you for being too desirable.'

The hoarseness of his voice excited me as much as his hands had and I felt my nipples hardening. His breathing quickened as he watched them respond. His lips parted slightly and then he bent his head and took one in his mouth. I arched back against the wall as he caressed me.

The knocking on the door became more persistent. 'Tell them to go away,' I growled, reaching for the top of his pants. I undid the button and zip and pushed them down, wrestling them over his enormous erection.

He paused and winced, pulling away from me and looking down at his stomach. Blood had seeped through his bandages and shirt.

'Christ,' I said, staring at it. 'Oh Roger, I'm so sorry.'

'Don't be,' he said, pulling me back to him.

'We can't,' I said. 'I don't want to hurt you.' My body was on fire for him, yearning to have him touch me again, but I pulled the robe shut and stepped away from him. 'Not till you're better,' I said.

He ran a hand through his hair in apparent frustration. 'I can't open the door like this,' he said, gesturing at himself.

It *was* an awfully impressive erection. 'Pull up your pants,' I said in my sternest voice, 'and go open that door before they come to the conclusion we're both dead.'

I pushed him out of the bathroom and locked the door so I could dress in privacy.

Christ. I didn't know how I was going to appear even slightly normal in front of the others. I should have been hysterical or in shock, not totally turned on. Hopefully they would confuse my flushed cheeks with signs of anger.

By the time I was dressed Roger had advised Mark and Nathan that I had been helping him with his investigations on the Cross Killer and that it was possible the dead bunny was a message from him. There wasn't really any more information I could give them.

They left shortly afterwards and as soon as the door had shut Roger pulled me into him, kissing me hungrily. Jeez, the man was the King of Kissing. I'm not sure if it was the way he moved his lips, or if they just happened to be a perfect fit for mine, but when he kissed me I became dizzy and disorientated. I felt like one of the actresses in the old black and white movies, swooning at his touch.

The only thing that gave me the strength to stop was the sight of the blood on his shirt.

'Stop,' I said, as he lifted up my blouse and undid my bra. 'We can't.'

He stopped and looked at me, panting slightly. Seeing him pant nearly undid me. I mean I didn't want him to stop till we were both naked and sweaty and sated. But he was hurt.

'Not until you've healed,' I said, doing up my bra.

Now that we had crossed the line I knew it would be impossible to be alone in private without us trying to jump each other's bones. 'Come on,' I said, 'I'll take you home.'

'What about the car?'

'Feel like going through a car wash.'

His face lit up with a naughty smile.

'Forget it,' I said, 'I'll call you a cab.'

Chapter Eleven

Comedy – Thy Name
Is Chanel

I was putting the finishing touches to my make-up when I heard the knock on my front door. I wasn't taking any chances since the bunny incident so I checked the peephole to make sure it was Martine and Ronnie before I opened it.

The three of us were walking to the club together. Mum was already there making last minute touches to the stage decorations. The judges from Las Vegas would be there tonight to mark their performance and she was leaving nothing to chance.

'Woo woo,' Martine said, looking me up and down. Then she clutched her stomach and sprinted for my bathroom.

'She's got the trots,' Ronnie informed me, moving a bit closer. 'I love that colour on you.'

I was wearing a teal green dress with black high heels. 'The shop assistant said it made my eyes pop.'

She moved closer and gazed at my face. 'That's not all it makes pop,' she purred.

She ran her hand down my dress and then back up to the bodice. We stood like that for a few seconds before I said, 'Ahh Ronnie, your hand seems to be on my breast.'

'Oh silly me,' she said. But she didn't move it.

Martine staggered out of the bathroom still clutching her belly. 'Ronnie,' she barked, 'leave Chanel alone.'

Ronnie pushed out her lower lip but she took her hand away and moved to the lounge.

'Sorry love,' Martine said, 'she still likes girls.' Her eyes widened and then she backed back into the bathroom and slammed the door shut.

I moved over to sit on the far end of the lounge from Ronnie. 'So does that make you gay or straight?' I said.

'Straight... I think.' She burst out laughing.

'How long has Martine had the trots?'

'All afternoon. She had prawns for lunch.'

I walked over to the bathroom trying to ignore the noises coming from within. 'Martine,' I yelled, 'there's some Imodium in my vanity bag under the sink. Take a couple.'

She emerged a few minutes later, looking pale and sweaty. 'Geez those tablets are big.'

'They're capsules,' I said.

'The two big tablets in the side pocket of your vanity.'

'In a box marked Imodium?'

'No by themselves.' She slumped on the couch moaning gently. 'Hope they work fast.'

I ran into the bathroom and grabbed my vanity bag, searching frantically through its contents.

'I think they are going to work faster than you'd like,' I said, coming back into the lounge. 'They weren't Imodium.'

'What were they?

As if on cue there was a soft ripping noise and Martine let out a yelp of pain. Her tight lycra skirt started to move of its own accord, rising into the air till it stood like a tent with its pole fully erect.

'Viagra.'

'Ahhhhh,' she shrieked, trying to push the tent down. It popped straight back up at full attention.

Ronnie pointed at Martine's erection and started to laugh. Tears rolled down her face as she gasped and chortled. Martine put her hands over it and turned to the side, but the floor lamp cast a long shadow on the wall next to her, amplifying the size of our problem.

'Stop it, oh stop it,' Ronnie screeched, beating her leg with her hand.

I couldn't help it; I started to laugh as well. The more she tried to hide it, the worse it got. I collapsed on the couch next to Ronnie, howling with laughter.

'It's not funny,' Martine cried.

'I know it's not.' Tears ran freely down my cheeks.

'Brings a whole new meaning to pole dancing doesn't it?' Ronnie said. She *really* wasn't helping the situation.

'Maybe we can strap it down,' I suggested.

'It *was* strapped down.'

'How much did she take?' Ronnie asked.

'Two hundred milligrams.'

'I'm screwed,' Martine said, sitting down on the couch.

The sight of her fully blown erection pushing up through the lycra was too much and Ronnie and I started laughing again.

'I'm sorry,' I said, wiping tears away, 'I know this isn't funny.'

'It is too,' Ronnie said.

Martine turned to me and clutched my hands. 'You have to do it,' she said.

'Do what?' I asked.

'The pole dance. I can't go out there like this.'

'Heelllooo boys,' Ronnie said.

'I can't do it,' I said.

'Yes you can. You know it.'

'Knowing and doing are two different things.'

'Please,' she said, clutching my hands. 'Please.' Tears welled up in her eyes and she started to cry. It wasn't pretty. 'You have to, you have to.'

She was working her way steadily towards hysteria and it was going to take forever to fix her make-up.

'What about Mum?'

'We need her down the front,' Ronnie said.

'Chaaannneeellll,' Martine howled, 'you have to.'

'Okay,' I said, more to placate her than anything. 'We'll see what Mum says. Maybe they won't notice if you're missing.'

'You'll do it if we need you?' she said, staring into my face. Her false eyelashes had come loose and were drooping over her eyes.

'Yes of course,' I said, hoping to hell that they wouldn't need me. 'Now come on, let's get you fixed up.

***

Mum stared at Martine's erection. 'Maybe you could wear a ruffled skirt,' she said.

'I won't be able to climb the pole. It'll get in the way.'

'You'll have to do it,' she said, turning to me.

'Me?'

'You know the dance.'

'I've never climbed the pole.'

'You know the theory.'

'It's not that hard,' Martine said.

A small smile formed on Bianca's face. 'It looks pretty hard from here.'

I looked at the tall shiny poles while trying to control the dizziness that was threatening to overcome me. My Mum wanted me to cut my pole dancing teeth in a competition? She was a maniac.

'Do we need someone on that pole? I asked.

'Yes, the competition minimum for any act is ten. We've only got nine without Martine.'

Great. Only nine other people for me to hide behind. 'What about the other girls?'

'They don't know the routine like you do. Ronnie, can you take Chanel back and get her into a costume.'

'I'll do it,' Martine said to my great relief. I still hadn't forgotten the feel of Ronnie's hand on my breast.

Ten minutes later I looked at myself in the mirror and said, 'You're kidding right?'

I was wearing a tiny sequined bra and matching lycra hot pants. They were bright pink.

'It's the only one that will fit you,' Martine said.

'You're sure this isn't some kind of payback?'

Martine smiled. 'I haven't even begun to pay you back.'

'Great,' I said, 'one more thing to be worried about.'

'Don't be worried, you look hot.'

'I'm worried about falling off the pole and getting a concussion.'

Mum was talking to the stage hand when we got back. She glanced over at me and said, 'You need to do more sit-ups.'

'Do you want me to do this or not?'

She laughed and turned back to her conversation.

'I was thinking black and with a little more material, but hey, it's your super hero costume.'

'I'm not cat woman,' I said to Bianca.

'Nope, tonight you're pole woman - saving a group of drag queens from certain disqualification.'

I would have laughed if I weren't feeling ill. The stress of the last few days was catching up with me and my palms were sweating and my knees were trembling. Ahhh, who am I kidding? It had nothing to do with the last few days. I was shit scared about performing in front of a crowd of people.

'Deep breaths,' Martine said as she led me up to the stage. 'So you start by walking around the pole once then you go into a fireman's twirl.'

'Can't I just crouch down at the back so no-one can see me?'

'Going to look pretty stupid when the rest of them are up the pole.'

I sighed. 'So what comes after the fireman's twirl?'

'You tell me.'

I let the music play in my head. 'Then a fan kick, and a spin and then into a front hook spin all the way to the ground,' I said.

'Right, that's the easy bit. Then climb and climb and…'

'Dying swan,' I said.

'Into a flying carpet and then slide down the pole. After that you freestyle - stalk around the pole and do the occasional spin. Ronnie will sing, and the front two rows will break off to dance so it's just the three of you at the back still on the poles.

'Anything else?'

'Point your toes and smile.'

I stuck my tongue out at her but didn't get a chance to say anything because the rest of the girls came onto the stage and took up their positions. *Yikes.* It was about to start.

I heard the chatter in the audience fade with the lights, until there was total silence. I concentrated on breathing as the curtain slid up; the bright lights almost blinding me as I stood in my high heels and slut outfit and smiled. And then the music began.

The irony of dancing to 'I Will Survive' was not lost on me. I strutted around the pole and did a fireman's twirl and by the front spin to the floor I was almost enjoying myself.

That all stopped as soon as I started trying to climb the pole. I grasped it with my hands and jumped up as I'd seen the girls do, wrapping my legs and feet around it. It really hurt. I grasped further up the pole and pushed with my feet while I pulled with my arms. I didn't go very far. I repeated the manoeuvre again and again, frantically inching my way up the pole. The girls were way ahead of me, almost at the roof, and I was visible through their legs as I huffed and puffed and pushed and pulled.

I could see Mum making climb faster actions, and then she may have made a you're dead motion. That only made my hands start to sweat, and of course then I wasn't going anywhere. I made a pretty good dying swan as I hung exhausted from the pole.

The real trouble came when I tried the magic carpet. The aim for this move is to make yourself horizontal on the pole. You lie back with your legs out straight and hang on with one hand and your thighs. The other hand is raised elegantly above your head. Well that's the aim anyway.

My magic carpet didn't quite work out that way. I got into the horizontal part, but I was having trouble maintaining my grip with my sweaty palms. One second I was horizontal and feeling pretty proud of myself, the next I lost my grip. Immediately my body tilted backwards and my legs pivoted upwards till I was hanging upside down on the pole.

The girls above me were holding their magic carpets perfectly as I found myself speeding head first towards the ground. Panicked, I threw my arms out and caught myself in a perfect handstand. All my schoolyard playing paid off and I flicked through a cartwheel till I was in a standing position. I stuck my arms out as if I was an Olympian gymnast and put a huge smile on my face. I was guessing by the way the crowd broke out into a huge round of applause that they hadn't heard my terrified shrieks as I'd slid down the pole.

Then I pranced and twirled around the pole while Ronnie sang and the other girls danced and finally, finally it was over. I staggered off the stage and collapsed at the bar, too buggered to care that I still had on the stupid outfit.

Bruce handed me a drink, a huge grin on his face, and then rushed off to serve other customers. I pressed the icy glass to my forehead before taking a gulp.

'Dang girl,' Bianca said, 'that was some serious shit. I thought you was gone for sure.'

'I was expecting a trip to the emergency ward.' I skolled the last of my drink and then looked down at my bare legs. 'I'm going to get changed.'

Martine was in the change rooms helping the girls with their costumes. She was wearing a longer skirt which helped hide her third leg. 'The real Imodium's finally kicked in.'

'You all right to go on?' I said.

'I'll stay in the background and make sure I don't cast a shadow.'

'Good luck,' I said and went back to the bar to enjoy the show.

They had been good when I first discovered Dazzle, but under Mum's tuition they had improved and I realised that they might be in with a chance to win the competition. Obviously I had no idea what the other troupes were like, but they would have to be excellent to beat the girls – that was if my stunt hadn't ruined it for them.

We didn't get home till it was almost sunrise. I took Cocoa out for a toilet break and then crawled into bed with him. It was almost too hot to cuddle, but I held on to him and tried not to think about the terrifying few seconds when I'd thought it was him on the bonnet of my car.

My mind switched to Roger as I was sliding off to sleep, and I had confusing dreams in which I fled from a shadowy figure while searching for Roger and Cocoa. I woke exhausted after the sun had risen, kicked off the covers and managed to fall into a dreamless sleep.

***

'No,' I said into the phone, 'not until you're better.'

Roger had rung me to try and convince me to come round to his. I knew what he was after, and even though I desperately wanted it too I was determined not to intervene with his body's attempts to heal.

'What if we meet on neutral ground?' He was persistent.

'Define neutral.'

'A restaurant.'

I thought about it for a few moments but couldn't come up with any reasons why we couldn't do that. 'Which restaurant?'

'Fook Yuen.'

'Well there's no need to be rude about it.'

He chuckled softly. 'It's a Chinese restaurant.'

'Oh.'

I jotted down the address and the time, glad I only had to wait a few days to see him. Work seemed like a rainy day without him there.

'I miss you,' he said.

I flushed with pleasure and looked around to see if Dave and Daniel could hear me. 'I miss you too,' I whispered. I hung up and went to the toilet to give myself time for the pink of my cheeks to dissipate.

'Ahh, young love,' Dave said when I came back out.

Damn, so he had been able to hear. 'Fook Yuen,' I said.

He let out a whistle and nodded his head. 'Flash. Make sure he springs for the Peking Duck.

Before he could say anything else Bob stuck his head through the door. 'Dave, need you out the front.'

I breathed a sigh of relief as he left to help Bob.

***

I ran into Marty when I got home. He was coming down the stairs from his apartment.

'Urrr hi,' I said. Things were always hard with Marty, but for Martine's sake I put in a good effort.

'Hi,' he said in his dull monotone voice.

'Um so ahh, how long did it take for things to return to normal.' I looked pointedly at his crutch.

'Next morning,' he said.

'Sorry about that.'

'You meant well.'

'Well, better go get Cocoa,' I said, shuffling to one side.

He moved at the same time and we found ourselves still blocking each other. Then we both moved the other way. Great, like things weren't awkward enough.

Waving an arm to the side I said, 'After you.'

I made it to my floor before I heard Mum's voice filtering down the stairs. 'Ooh Joe, you shouldn't have.'

I sighed and hurried into my apartment before I heard more than I wanted to.

Cocoa was excited to see me, jumping all over me for a few minutes before running over to sit beneath his lead. I clipped him on and went down to the park where Bruce was waiting.

'When do you find out about the comp?' I said, taking a seat next to him.

'End of the month.'

'Do you think I screwed up their chances?'

He laughed. 'On the contrary the judges loved the comedy act.' He made quotation marks with his fingers when he said the last bit.

'Comedy, thy first name is Chanel,' I said.

'Coming down tonight?'

'Nah. Need a quiet night in.'

'Don't answer your door to anybody and keep your mobile with you.'

'I've started bringing my gun home,' I whispered.

He stared at me for a second. 'You can do that?'

'We keep them in lockers. No-one checks.'

'But you'd be in trouble if you got caught.'

'With my current track record I'd be kicked off the Force.'

'Better that,' he said.

I swallowed as I imagined my body lying in an alley, throat slit, soaked in my own blood. Yes, better being kicked off the Force than that. Hopefully they weren't my only options.

***

It's a sad state of affairs when you find yourself deliberating between two minute noodles and curry in a hurry, but that's what I was doing when there was a knock at my door. I grabbed my gun from the kitchen table and peered through the peep hole. It was Mum. I hid the gun in my handbag before letting her in.

'Want to go out for dinner?' she asked. Her perfume wafted into the room ahead of her, heavy and expensive.

'Weren't you out with Joe?'

'Just a drink. Thought it would be nice to have some one-on-one time with my daughter.'

'Bruce told you about the rabbit.' It was a statement not a question.

'I'm worried about you.'

'Not as worried as I am,' I mumbled.

'My shout and you can fill me in.'

I had never said no to a free dinner and now didn't seem like the right time to break that tradition. Besides, it would be nice to share my burden. I hadn't told her because I didn't want to worry her, but now that she knew, I found I wanted to tell her everything.

I had never noticed the restaurant she took me to. A small Italian pizzeria tucked away between a hairdresser's and a butcher. The smells coming out of it made me realise how hungry I was.

I told her everything. About finding the cigars and then Rosie being killed, about Lizette coming to see me but running away before I could help. About the tobacconist and the fire and Roger being burnt, and finally about the horror of the rabbit and the personal threat.

She knew a lot of it already, but it was good to tell it as a cohesive whole. It put it all together for me, making it seem more real and less of a nightmare.

'So this Roger,' she said, 'what's the deal there?'

I grimaced. 'Not sure, early days.'

'But you like him?'

'I like him too much,' I admitted. 'He makes me feel...' I paused while I tried to put a finger on it. 'Alive,' I finished.

'Alive is good,' she said as she put some money on the table. 'Let's try and keep it that way.'

We were half way home when her mobile rang. She pulled it out of her pocket and glanced at the screen before answering.

'Speaking,' she said. 'I'm sorry, who is this?'

She was silent as she listened. Then she held a hand up, pulled a sorry face and moved further up the road to talk in private. I leaned back against the building and watched her as I pondered who she could be talking to.

That was why I didn't see the man walking up the road until he was right in front of me. I let out an instinctive yelp and jumped away from the building getting ready to defend myself. The man stopped walking and looked at me.

I pressed a hand to my chest, feeling the racing beat of my heart and said, 'You scared me.'

As he watched me I realised it was a bit warm to be wearing the black jumper he had on, especially with the hood up. His face was shadowed by it as he stood ominously, quietly. And then he said, 'Chanel?'

'I'm sorry, do I know you?' I backed away into the wall of the building and glanced up the street, but Mum had her back to me, waving an arm around as she spoke into the phone.

'Chanel Smith?' The words were laced with danger.

The light of a passing car illuminated his face under the hood for a split second, burning the image into my mind. Piercings covered him; multiple bars through his eyebrows, a ring through the middle of his nose, and another each side of his lower lip. A tattoo wrapped around his neck and trailed up onto his left cheek. But that wasn't the scary part, that wasn't the part that had me rifling blindly through my handbag searching for my gun. His eyes burned black and hard. Hatred and rage and pain mingled together as he glared at me.

'Lizette told me about you,' he said, stepping towards me.

A vision of Lizette as I had last seen her flashed into my head and I let out a shriek. My right hand dug desperately into the contents of my bag, feeling and discarding object after object in its search for cold metal.

'Don't come any closer,' I panted, wondering what it would feel like to have my throat slit.

'Or what?' His voice was hard and angry.

My hand closed on cold and hard, but it wasn't my gun. I pulled it out of my bag, yanked off the lid and squirted him in the eyes with my perfume.

'Jesus Christ,' he shrieked, clutching his face. 'What was that?'

'Chanel number five,' I said as I kicked him in the balls. He dropped to his knees, one hand on his face, the other on his crutch.

'Don't move a fucking inch,' Mum said.

She was standing with her feet shoulder width apart and her arms stretched out straight. There was a gun clasped tightly in her hands.

'Where the hell did you get that from?' I said, staring at the gun. It was huge.

'My handbag.' It wasn't the answer I was looking for but it surprised me anyway. How had she managed to fit that thing in her clutch?

'Pyscho bitch,' the guy gasped. 'I just wanted to talk.'

'Yeah right.' I pulled my cuffs out of my bag. 'I've heard that one before.' I hadn't really but I enjoyed saying it. Made me feel like I was a character in a movie and not being stalked by a real life serial killer.

I read him his rights and pulled his hands behind his back while Mum kept her gun trained on him. 'You better put that thing away before the cops get here,' I said, pulling my phone out.

'Why?' she said. 'I've got a licence.'

Holy shit, what parallel universe had I slipped into? My mother had a gun licence?

'When did you get that?'

'About twenty five years ago.'

The significance of the timing was not lost on me. Mum had gotten a gun licence while still pregnant with me. One of these days we were going to have a really, really long talk.

I called the station and spoke to Jake, and he promised a car was on its way.

'I didn't do nothin' wrong?' Tattoo Face said.

'You realise that means you did something wrong?' Mum said to him. 'The correct statement would be I didn't do *anything* wrong.' She turned to me and shook her head. 'I don't know what they teach kids in schools these days.'

I was still a bit freaked out. Some guy had tried to attack me and my Mum was carrying a gun.

'What is that thing?' I said, pointing at her gun.

'44 Magnum. Same as Dirty Harry.' She smiled broadly.

Correction, my mother was carrying a 44 Magnum. The only Magnums I'd ever carried were covered in chocolate.

True to Jake's word the boys in blue arrived a few minutes later. Dave climbed out of the passenger's side.

'What are you doing here?' I asked.

'Extra shift.'

He looked at Tattoo Face, who had assumed a cross legged position on the ground. 'Jesus Chanel,' he said, 'you're some kind of weird shit magnet.'

'Tell me about it,' Mum said. 'You should have seen the losers she used to date.'

'They were bad boys, not losers,' I said.

'Hmphhh. The only thing bad about them was their haircuts. I think that's why she was drawn to hairdressing.'

Dave had a huge grin on his face. 'You must be Mrs Smith.'

'Ohh, please call me Lorraine.' And then she fluttered her eyelids at him. It was a bit hard to tell with it being so dark but I was almost certain he blushed.

I had a hard look at Mum. I had managed to ignore the fact for quite a while now, what with her being my mother and my inability to see past the creature I had known for most of my life, but I had to admit that the woman she was now was smoking hot. Chin length red hair, a polka-dot black and white silk blouse teamed with knee length pants that hugged a rockin' body and fire engine red heels that matched her Magnum-holding clutch.

Yikes, it was possible I was being out classed by my mother. I hadn't changed my hair colour for months and I couldn't remember the last time I'd even window-shopped. Granted, I'd been a little preoccupied with the serial killer in my life, but that was no excuse. The stakes had been raised and I was going to have to step up to the mark.

Once Dave and his partner, Rick, had taken Tattoo Face off to the station, Mum and I continued our walk home. We didn't speak and a lot of the time we were looking backwards, not forwards, but we made it home safely. Mum came in and collapsed on the couch, much to Cocoa's delight.

'That was intense,' she said. 'You need to get a gun.'

'I had one,' I said.

'Well why the hell did you spray him with your perfume?'

'I couldn't find it.'

She looked at my enormous handbag. 'Say no more. What are you carrying?'

'Glock.'

'The one you were issued with?'

I nodded my head.

'It's good to know you're packing, even if you couldn't find it.'

'Ahh Mum,' I said, 'how do you know these things?'

'What things?'

'That I was issued with a Glock.'

'Google.'

'Oh.' I didn't know what I was expecting, certainly not something so rational.

She patted me on the arm. 'Got to get my beauty sleep, got a date tomorrow night.'

'Joe?'

'I could tell you, but I'd have to shoot you.' She laughed and hopped up off the couch.

'I've got a date as well,' I said.

'Roger?'

'I could tell you, but I'd have to spray you in the face with my perfume.'

She chuckled and then kissed me on the cheek. 'Stay safe,' she said as she left.

Stay safe. I really wanted to. I was tired of being scared all the time. There was, however, a possibility we had just apprehended the killer.

I felt a small measure of relief at the thought, and also at the knowledge that by the time I got to work I would have more information. But still I tossed and turned in my sleep, pursued by a shadow man thirsting for my blood, and I was glad when my alarm finally went off in the morning.

Chapter Twelve

Some Days Aren't Worth Getting Out Of Bed For

I was surprised to see Trent out the back making a coffee when I got to work the next morning.

'Drug dealing not working out for you?' I said as I put my bag on my desk.

'Cover got blown.'

'By me?' I squeaked.

He let out a deep chuckle. 'No. We made a bust last week, got one of the major players but my cover was blown. I'm filling in here till Roger's back.'

'Oh well congrats and commiserations,' I said.

'Been meaning to apologise for the shit you got into when you arrested me.'

'Apologising for making a lousy drug dealer?'

'No.' He paused. 'Well, it was unfair what happened.'

Everyone kept saying that. Everyone except Ramy. And he was the only one whose opinion mattered.

I shrugged a shoulder. 'Just don't do it again.'

He snapped a salute. 'Yes Maam.'

Oh great, a smartass.

I made myself a coffee and was surprised to find him sitting on the edge of my desk when I got back. He was so tall that the desk was almost uncomfortably short for him as a perch.

'I interviewed your man,' he said.

'Tattoo Face? He's still here?'

'We had to let him go.' He sounded frustrated.

'You didn't have any reason to hold him?'

'Judge Pierce refused to sign the search warrant until this morning.'

'What did you get a search warrant for?' I took a seat and peered up at him.

'Turns out he was their pimp.'

'Pardon?'

'All the girls that were killed, he was their pimp.'

I felt my mouth dry and my pulse speed up. Their pimp? 'Why would he kill his means of income?'

Trent raised both shoulders. 'After we got the warrant we searched his apartment. We found a shirt in the wash. It had blood on it.'

'Could be anyone's blood,' I said, but I was feeling light headed.

'That's what I thought. Put it straight in for forensics, we should have the results this afternoon.' He stood up and headed back out the front, leaving his dirty coffee cup sitting on my desk. Typical bloody detective.

I passed the day in a state of high nerves, partly because of my date that night and partly because we potentially knew the identity of the serial killer. We were all hanging on the results of that shirt and when it came back positive for Lizette's blood I sat down and put my head between my legs.

'You all right?' Daniel asked.

'Uhuh,' I said, wondering if there was a paper bag anywhere in the station. Was it possible it was over? Would I really be able to live my life without having to look over my shoulder?

'He'll be singing a different tune,' Trent said when he came out for more coffee.

'You've got him?'

'Not yet.'

'How do you think he knew who I was?'

'He knew that Lizette came to you for help. Maybe he followed her.'

'He told you that?'

'Said she told him she came to you because she saw the killer.'

That was weird. Why would Lizette tell him she'd come to me if he really were the killer?

'He said that she saw the killer come in while she was here and ran away.'

I stared at him. 'She saw the killer here?'

'That's what he said.'

'Well he was obviously lying.'

'Probably.'

'Trying to deflect the heat.'

'Possibly.'

Daniel had wandered over to my table to listen in on the conversation. 'If only we had DNA to tie him to the crime scene,' he said.

I smacked myself in the head. 'But we do,' I yelped. Jesus where was my head at? So much had happened since the fire had led to a dead end, I had forgotten about the cigar butts.

They looked at me blankly. 'The butts,' I said.

'Whose butt?' Trent said.

I'd forgotten he hadn't been here for the majority of the investigation.

'The cigar butts Roger and I found at the scenes.' I thought it only fair that I get a little of the credit. They both looked at me blankly. 'The Hula Girl cigar butts.'

Trent burst out laughing. 'You're pulling my leg?'

I shook my head. 'No seriously. We found one at every scene. They all came back with the same DNA on them. We just never had anyone to check it against.'

Trent tensed, his limbs going from long and relaxed to coiled, like a feline predator ready to pounce. 'Daniel, find the DNA results,' he said. 'They should be in the register.'

He was gone as soon as he'd finished speaking, leaving his empty coffee cup on my desk, again.

'What do you think he's doing?' I said.

'Getting a warrant to obtain DNA from the suspect.'

'Oh yeah. Right. Hey how did they get the blood results back so quickly? I thought it normally took days.'

'More like weeks,' he said. 'A serial killer is a priority case. The DNA testing can be done in a few hours, but there's a huge backlog.'

'How do you know that?' I asked. I was pretty sure we hadn't covered that at the Academy. And I certainly hadn't come across it during my studies since.

'I've got a degree in forensic science.'

'Wow. What are you doing here?'

'Thought I could make more of a difference on this end.'

'How's that working out for you?'

He laughed and headed back to his desk. 'When I'm a detective it'll work out just fine.'

Damn, the man had a ten-year plan. I didn't have a ten-day one.

They still hadn't found Tattoo Face when I left work that afternoon. I was already running late, having to write up some paperwork on a flasher Mark and I had brought in, and only had an hour before I had to meet Roger.

'Chanel,' Daniel called as I headed out the door.

I thought about pretending I hadn't heard him, but with his sincerity and those coke bottle glasses I just couldn't lie to the guy. 'Yes,' I said, sticking my head back through the door.

'I can't find those DNA results.'

'Huh?'

'The cigar butts. I can't find them in the register.'

'They were nearly a month ago,' I said.

'I've gone right back to when we got here.' He pushed his glasses up his nose making his eyes appear huge in comparison to the rest of his face.

'I'm seeing Roger in an hour,' I said. 'I'll ask him where they are.'

He smiled in relief and nodded his head.

'You staying?'

'Extra shift.'

Huh, why was I the only one not getting extra shifts? Not that I wanted to work a double shift. But the fact that I wasn't getting them stunk of...well I wasn't sure what it stunk of, but it stunk of something.

'Okay,' I said, 'I'll ring in the information.'

As I walked home I considered driving to the Fook Yuen. My internal dialogue went as follows:

If we drive we can spend an extra fifteen minutes doing our hair.

But if we drive we'll have to count our drinks.

Maybe that's not such a bad thing – you know.

I know what?

Well if we drink too much we may not say no if he asks to walk us home.

I'm counting on him walking us home. It's dangerous out there. And besides, it'll mean we get to spend more time with him.

That's true.

And he can kiss us good night on the doorstep.

That would be romantic.

Well that's settled then. We walk.

And we say no.
Of course.

I've always been a bit of a pushover.

***

There was a handbag sitting by my door when I got home with a note on it. I picked it up and read the note.

This is a much better size. Love Mum.

Although it was a gorgeous shiny coral it was smaller than my other handbags. How was I going to fit everything in? But I guess that was the point. I was going to have to cull so there'd be fewer things to get in between my hand and my gun when I needed it the most.

I rushed the shower, took my time with my hair and makeup, and then threw on a little black Ralph Lauren dress. The shoes took me longer to decide on. Sexy or sensible? I resented the choice and was looking forward to not having to consider the negative implications of my sexy shoes. But as it was I strapped on my sensible shoes with a sigh. At least they were black.

I tipped the contents of my bag onto my bed and sorted through it, reluctantly putting aside the hairspray, four lipsticks, my spare brush, some clips and bobby pins, one of the bottles of perfume and my compact mirror. Into the new bag went my wallet, gun, phone, handcuffs, perfume, lip gloss, baby wipes and at last second I threw the compact mirror back in. I was counting the perfume as a weapon – if I wasn't close enough to spray it I could always throw it.

By the time I had done that I only had ten minutes to get to the restaurant. I ran down the stairs, feeling smug about my sensible shoes, and up the street.

I'm still not sure if it was my incredible good luck or my incredible bad luck that allowed me to hear the noise. If I hadn't paused in the mouth of the alley next to the Fook Yeun, digging around my gun and hand cuffs for my dusty pink luscious lips lip balm, at the precise moment there was a total absence of traffic noise – which in itself is a rare and unusual thing – I wouldn't have heard it at all. As it was, with only the noise of my own frustrated breathing I barely heard it.

A muffled scream cut off abruptly into a low gurgle. It made the hair on the back of my neck stand up on end. I licked my still balmless lips nervously and looked around for a police officer before remembering that shit, I *was* a police officer. Sighing, I recommenced my digging, this time pulling out my Glock and taking it off safety.

I felt only marginally better with the weapon in my hand. It's one thing to have a gun but you still have to aim straight, and that had never been my strength at the Academy. But I started off down the alley, wishing it weren't so dark, and that my heart wasn't beating quite so fast. I was scared. I don't think I'd ever been that scared before. My hands were clammy and my steps trembled, but I fixed the dead faces of Leticia, Rosie and Lizette in my mind and I continued down the alley.

If I were correct in my assumption, I was willingly walking through the dark towards a ruthless and merciless killer. The Chanel of a year ago would have turned tail and run, as it was I barely managed to keep myself going. The urge to flee was overwhelming.

The heavy traffic noise had recommenced behind me and I felt cut off from the rest of the world. No-one would hear my scream and come to my rescue if this didn't go well. I could see the end of the alley, the walls lined with rubbish dumpsters from the restaurants surrounding us. Dim light emitted from those same restaurants, illuminating some areas, but throwing much into shadow. Faint music and exotic scents that normally would have made my mouth water tumbled into the alley. I was too scared to be hungry, too scared to feel anything but the deep, dark paralysis of fear creeping into my mind and limbs.

I inched further down the alley, my arms held out in front of me, my finger on the trigger. And then I started to think. Why was I here? Why was I alone? Even though I'd made good time to the restaurant Roger would have been there already. I could go back and get him and we could call for backup. Chances were the noise I had heard was nothing; the cry of a cat in a fight.

I had started to turn when I saw her body lying in a shaft of dim light. It was strewn across a pile of garbage someone had been too lazy to put into a dumpster.

I tried to convince myself she was a homeless person asleep in the alley, but I knew different. It had been her cry I heard from the street. The last sound she ever made had reached my ears. Clenching my courage around me like a cloak I moved towards her.

Of all the dead bodies I'd seen, this one disturbed me the most. It wasn't the vacant eyes, or the ragged cut at her throat. It wasn't the blood pooled in her long blonde hair. It was the fact that I knew, somewhere in the dark shadows, the killer lay in wait.

The memory of Tattoo Face's hard glittering eyes haunted me. Was he watching me? Was he even now planning my death, imagining the feel of his blade slicing through my skin?

I held my gun with my left hand while I searched for my phone with my right. If I could ring Roger, tell him where I was, he could be here in under a minute. That thought was foremost in my mind when I heard a noise, a shoe scraping over rock, and I froze.

He *was* there. Watching me. I knew what a gazelle felt like when a lion approached. I wanted to flee, I wanted to scream, but my body wouldn't move. An involuntary whimper came out of my mouth.

What had I been thinking? I was no match for a psychopath.

Another noise – rustling - came from back down the alley. *Good God.* I'd walked past him. Right past him.

The noises continued. Coming closer. Each one winding me tighter and tighter. I stared towards the sounds, terror bubbling inside, horror crawling over my skin. A shadow morphed in the alley taking on human form. A scream formed in my chest, worked its way raggedly up to my throat and then Roger stepped out of the shadows.

I sagged, dropping my gun back in my bag and starting to cry. 'Thank God it's you,' I said, walking towards him.

'Who did you think it would be?'

'Look.' I gestured towards the woman.

'Oh dear,' he said, 'not another one.' And then he pulled out a cigar and lit it with a glove covered hand.

It took a few seconds for the synapses in my brain to connect the dots. When they did the horror was almost too much.

'You,' I panted, unable to comprehend it. 'You?'

'Poor sweet Chanel,' he said, walking towards me. 'So trusting, so desirable.' He ran a hand down my cheek and I shuddered and backed away.

'Don't touch me,' I said.

'Or what? You'll scream?' I could see his sneer in the dim light from the restaurant.

'No,' I said, taking my gun back out of my bag, 'I'll shoot.' I tried to sound brave, but my voice shook, and my hand trembled. Even though I was the one holding the gun I was terrified.

He backed away from the barrel as he shook his head. 'Tsk, tsk, Chanel,' he said. 'You brought your gun home from work.'

'If you didn't want me to start carrying my gun around you shouldn't have sacrificed a rabbit on the bonnet of my car.' I took my phone out of my bag and waved him towards the end of the alley, away from any chance of escape. I really didn't want to try and shoot him if he fled.

'How did you do that?' I asked. He raised an eyebrow at me and suddenly all the pieces of the puzzle clicked into place. 'That's why you said you'd meet me out the front of the hospital,' I said. 'You'd already been released.'

'Clever, clever,' he said.

'I don't know how you thought you were going to do this and still meet me for dinner.'

His smile hardened, taking on a vicious edge. 'Oh Chanel, you were never going to make it to dinner.'

'Why me?' I felt ill. Discussing why Roger wanted to kill me had not been in my plans for this evening.

'You're far too curious for your own good.'

And then I really understood. 'The killer in London you told me about, it was you, wasn't it?'

He smiled and raised the cigar to his lips. 'You're not as stupid as you look.'

His insult had an effect he hadn't considered. It helped turn my fear into anger. Don't get me wrong, I was still mind-numbingly terrified, but my limbs were no longer paralysed. Before I had felt like a mouse with a cat, now I had turned into a terrier.

'Hula Girl cigars?' I said.

He lifted the cigar, examined it and then shrugged his shoulders. 'What can I say? I like the coconutty flavour.'

'Why'd you have to kill the tobacconist?'

'His blood is on your hands, not mine.'

'How is that even possible?'

'If you hadn't stuck your pretty little nose into the case I wouldn't have had to shut down the lead.'

I felt sullied. Manipulated and sullied. I had admired this man and, if I was totally honest, had been falling in love with him. All this talk made no difference. He was a psychopath and it wasn't my job to try and make him see the error of his ways. It was, however, my job to stop him.

'Tell that to the judge,' I said, shaking my head. I looked down at my phone for a second, scrolled to work and hit the ring button. That second of distraction was all the time he needed.

He struck like a snake, his movements a blur to my peripheral vision. He grabbed my right arm and twisted rapidly, karate chopping the outside of my elbow.

I heard the crack a couple of seconds before my brain registered the pain. Two blissful seconds before agony raced from the wounded joint, ripping from my throat in a raw scream. The gun fell from my hand, my injured arm unable to support its weight.

Roger leapt forwards and kicked the gun away from me. I turned and ran, sprinting towards the road. My jolting steps banged my ruined arm against my side, bringing tears to my eyes.

If I thought I could have gotten away from him I was mistaken. He was much faster than me. He caught me by my ponytail and ripped me back, flinging me to the ground at his feet. I tried to stand but he kicked me in the stomach, and then smashed the back of his hand across my cheekbone.

I doubled over and fell, catching myself with my good hand, the phone falling from my fingers. My stomach protested at the rough treatment and I heaved a few times before rolling to the side and crawling to my feet. Before I could run he grabbed my damaged arm, wrenching the ends of the broken bone against each other as he threw me against a dumpster. I screamed with pain and felt a second crack as my back hit the hard metal. Sharp pain radiated through my chest making breathing almost impossible.

He pulled me upright with one hand, the fist of the other smacking into my cheek. My head snapped back and before I could recover, he slapped me as hard as he could.

'Nosey bitch,' he growled, slapping me again.

I shrieked and put my left arm up to protect my face. He moved to my stomach, punching me again and again until finally I collapsed onto the ground, my useless right arm collapsing under me. As I panted and cried and retched I saw the light glint off the metal of my gun. I rolled and lunged towards it with my left arm, feeling the cool metal slap into the palm of my hand just before he threw me back again. I landed with my back against the bin and shakily raised my left arm, the barrel of my Glock once again trained on his chest. He backed away, his arms held up.

For a second we stared into each other's eyes. I took pleasure in the shock that I saw there, the uncertainty. Then I pulled off the first shot without even thinking.

It wasn't at all like in training. In training I had been calm and collected, had had time to aim. I hadn't been terrified. My eyes hadn't been clouded with tears. I had been aiming at a piece of cardboard, not a real breathing person.

And of course in training my hand hadn't been shaking so hard that I missed the target totally.

Roger's laugh was evil, excited. 'Shoot me once shame on you,' he said.

I squeezed again, and missed.

'Shoot me twice shame on me.' He lashed out with his boot, smashing my head into the hard metal of the bin. Pain exploded through my mind and darkness threatened to take me. But I held on. I wasn't ready to die. Gripping the gun I raised it again, screaming hysterically as I fired again and again and again.

I missed him every time.

'Jesus Chanel,' he said, 'that's the worse bit of marksmanship I've ever seen.' He shook his head at me as I lay panting in the dirt at his feet. 'If I've been counting right, and I'm not sure if I have, you've fired 14 of your 15 shots. That leaves one.' He laughed quietly to himself before saying, 'Do you feel lucky punk? Well do you?'

'That's...my...line,' I said through gritted teeth, and then I aimed at his stomach and fired.

He had counted right, and the last of my bullets must have missed him by millimetres. I saw the look of triumph on his face. He threw back his head to laugh, and then he stopped. His eyes went blank, rolled back in his head and then he collapsed forwards on top of me.

Chapter Thirteen

What Doesn't Kill Us Makes Us Stronger – Or So They Say

When I came to, Roger's weight was pinning me to the ground. I screamed and fought, biting and clawing and then I realised he wasn't fighting back. I managed to shove him off me and I crawled to the side and threw up. My head was throbbing, my ribs were aching and I was still having trouble breathing. On a scale of one to ten my arm was a twenty.

It seemed like a good idea to have another little nap.

I could hear my name being called through the fog in my mind. It was distant and crackly and it sounded like Dave. I felt around on the ground, finally finding my phone, and I lifted it to my ear.

'Mmmm,' I said.

'Jesus Chanel.' It *was* Dave. 'Are you okay?'

'I hurt,' I said. And I started to cry.

'The boys are on their way. Where are you exactly?'

'In the alley,' I whispered.

'Behind the Fook Yuen?'

'Yes.' I put my head back down on the ground but kept my eyes open, trying to stay conscious. Tears trickled down my cheeks and onto the ground. It felt like forever in my world of pain before I could see the torch lights bobbing down the alley. I tried to stand up to meet them, but my body refused to co-operate.

'Over here.' My voice was pathetic.

'Christ,' Trent said, shining his torch on the dead woman. The light scanned around onto Roger before he finally found me. He knelt beside me and examined me in the torch light. 'You look like shit.'

'I've felt better,' I croaked.

'The ambulance is on the way,' he said.

'What happened to Detective Richardson,' Daniel asked.

'I tried to shoot him,' I said, 'but I missed.'

Trent snorted and shook his head. 'You're lucky to be alive.'

'Lucky unlucky,' I said. And then my brain decided to turn off for a while.

***

When I woke I was lying in a bed in a strange room. I gathered by the pristine white sheets that were tucked tightly around me that it was a hospital bed. Mum sat by me reading a book. She had on a full face of make-up and was wearing a low cut blue dress. The colour looked amazing against her fiery hair.

'Going somewhere?' I mumbled.

She dropped the book and smiled down at me as she held onto my hand. 'No just here with my hero daughter.'

I snorted. 'Hero Schmero. You're awfully dressed up for the hospital.'

'Never know when a cute doctor might walk by.'

'If anyone's getting the cute doctor it's me,' I said. I tried to sit up and winced. Wow, I really hurt.

'Careful darling,' she said. 'You're pretty banged up. I doubt you're going to get the doctor looking like that.'

She handed me a mirror and I automatically reached for it with my right hand. I stared in dismay at the cast that covered my entire arm.

'You had an operation,' she said. 'They had to put some pins in.'

I reached out my left hand and grasped the mirror. I had two black eyes and my nose was strapped and swollen. There was a large bandage wrapped around my head.

'I might get the pity vote,' I said, handing her the mirror. The image disturbed me more than I was letting on but there was no use crying over spilt milk, or in my case a split lip.

'That's the spirit,' she said. I got the feeling I hadn't fooled her.

'Detective Bailey rang earlier.'

'Detective Bailey?'

'Trent.'

'What did he want?'

'Well apparently they heard a lot of what went on through the phone - that was a stroke of brilliance darling - but he still needs to talk to you.'

I wasn't sure if I was ready to relive it yet; didn't know if I ever would be ready to relive it. I wasn't just physically battered I was emotionally destroyed. Someone I trusted had violated that trust in the worst possible way and I didn't know if that was something I was ever going to recover from.

I looked around and realised that vases of flowers covered every available surface in my room. 'Who?' I said, pointing at them.

'Ever since the news got out they've been turning up.'

'That's nice.' I closed my eyes and tried to go back to sleep but my mind had woken up even if my body didn't want to. There were a lot of unanswered questions. How long had I been unconscious? What had killed Roger? Where had Mum got that dress?

'Detective Bailey I assume,' I heard Mum say. I opened my eyes to see Trent stride into the room.

He had a small bunch of pansies in one hand and he stopped and stared at all the others flowers. 'Umm,' he said, 'these are from my garden.'

'I like a man who knows his flowers,' Mum purred, jumping up and taking them from him. She put them in a glass right beside the bed and sat back down, crossing her legs to reveal a length of brown thigh.

'Thanks,' I said. 'Trent, this is my Mum, Lorraine.' I tried to smile but my lips were too swollen to move much.

He nodded his head at her and then looked back at me, shaking his head. 'You look worse every time I see you.'

'You know how to make a gal feel special,' I said.

'You're lucky to be alive.'

'You said that last night.'

'And that was before I counted the spent shells.'

'I told you I missed him,' I murmured.

'Fifteen times? He was standing, what, two metres away? How is that even possible?'

'I was using my left hand. And it was trembling.' I tried to cross my arms, but the blasted cast got in the way totally ruining the effect. 'And I had my eyes closed.'

He burst out laughing. 'Your eyes were closed?'

'It was pretty scary; you had to be there to appreciate it.'

'Scary for the far wall,' he said. 'Anyway you only missed him 14 times. The last one rebounded off the dumpster hinge and hit him in the back of the head.'

'Pardon?'

'You shot him in the back of the head,' Mum said, standing up and leaning towards me so that Trent copped an eyeful of cleavage.

'Jolly good,' I said. I'd never realised how impressive her breasts were before. Between them and the head injury I was feeling pretty distracted.

'Anyway you're being given a VA and Ramy has reluctantly withdrawn your formal warnings.'

'That's big of him,' Mum said, leaning back against the bench behind her.

'Between us,' Trent said conspiratorially, 'the head honchos weren't too happy with him giving their shining star two formal warnings. They're looking into it even as we speak.'

'Isn't that good Chanel?' Mum turned to look at me.

'What about my gun?' I said. I mean surely I was going to pay for that. I was pretty sure that my career in the Police Force had finished in this blaze of glory.

'You mean your gun that I gave you permission to take with you when you followed a lead?'

I stared at him for a few seconds before his words sunk into my drug stupored head. *Wow*. He had covered for me.

My arm had started to ache with all the talk of shooting and the pain was increasing with each beat of my heart. 'Thank you,' I said, tears welling from the pain.

'You don't look so good.' Trent stared at me, concern etched his features.

'I feel awful,' I croaked. I was suddenly extremely tired, and sad. I felt like someone had died, and then I realised they had, and I felt even more tired and more sad. Combined with the pain, it was overwhelming and I wanted to dive deep into the unconsciousness I had only just returned from.

Mum hit the call button and within a handful of seconds a nurse had appeared by my bed. She seemed more interested in Trent than me, so I let out a pitiful moan.

'Goodness,' she said, suddenly the picture of efficiency. She left and was back shortly with a syringe which she injected into my intravenous line.

Almost immediately I started to feel better. The world took on a rosy, smudged glow.

'For the pain,' the nurse said to Mum. 'It'll make her drowsy.'

'Trent,' I said dreamily, wondering which of the two Trents I could see was the real one, 'what's a VA?'

'You can't remember?'

'I have a head injury.' I figured I may as well take advantage of my injuries while I could.

'It's the Valour Award, an in-service bravery decoration.'

'Oh,' I said. A tear slipped out of the corner of my eye and trailed lazily down my cheek.

Trent moved closer to Mum, and even through the fog starting to cover my mind it seemed weird, as though he was standing too close to someone he had only just met. He leant back against the bench behind them, his shoulder almost touching hers. She turned her face towards him and for a wild second I thought they were going to kiss. My heavy eyelids traitorously drifted shut of their own accord, and I could feel myself being drawn away from the room and reality.

Just before I passed out I distinctly heard Trent's voice. It sounded amused and a little frustrated as he said. 'So Tess, long time no see.'

And then my head was filled with white fuzz.

THE END

About Me

Hi there, I'm Donna Joy Usher. I started writing my first novel when I was seven. With no idea about plot or character development (I mean I *was* only seven) my storyline quickly disintegrated into a muddled jumble of boring dialogue between two horses.

Disillusioned, I gave up writing stories for quite a while after that. Instead, I concentrated on my studies, eventually graduating as a dentist.

After many years of 'drilling and filling' I turned to writing in an effort to escape the seriousness of my day job. During that time I created my first book, *The Seven Steps to Closure*, and discovered that I love nothing more than making other people laugh. Well that, and my two miniature schnauzers, Chloe and Ebony.

I currently live near the Swan River in the beautiful city of Perth. When I am not working or writing, I love to kayak, ride my bicycle, and sip chai lattes at the local cafe.

You can connect with me on Facebook (@authordonnajoyusher), Goodreads, Instagram (@donnajoyusher_theauthor), and my website donnajoyusher-theauthor.com

What To Read Next

Goons 'n' Roses
Book Two in
The Chanel Series

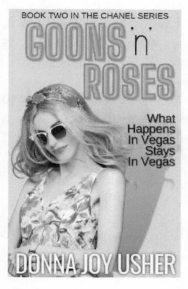

It's been 3 months since Chanel's world fell apart and now she's ready for a vacation. Unfortunately, her all-expenses-paid trip to Las Vegas is not turning out as she had hoped. Within hours of arriving her mum, Lorraine, is kidnapped. Then Trent, her boss and Lorraine's boyfriend, disappears; but not before he imparts information about an Interpol investigation into missing girls in Las Vegas.

When Chanel hooks up with local bad boy, the seriously sexy Billy, in a bid to get information, things only start to get worse. As she and Martine search for answers they are thwarted by obstacles and pursued by ruthless killers.

Who really kidnapped Lorraine? What happened to the missing girls? Can the delicious Billy be trusted? These are all questions that she needs to find the answers to, before the answers find her.

Follow this link to find out where you can purchase *Goons 'n' Roses*: https://donnajoyusher-theauthor.com/get-goons/

Tess's Tale
Book Three in
The Chanel Series

It's been twenty-five years since that hellish night. Twenty-five years of living in denial, and Tess still doesn't want to think about it. But now her daughter, Chanel, is insisting that she spill the beans.

So Tess must cast her mind back to a life of passion and betrayal, to a time of violence and death, and she must face her past to tell us… what really happened to Lou the Brain.

Visit https://donnajoyusher-theauthor.com/get-tess/ to view purchasing options.

The Seven Steps To Closure

Winner of the 2012 elit Publishing Award Humor Category.
Finalist in the 2012 Shirley You Jest Book Awards.
Finalist in the 2013 Indie Excellence Awards Chicklit Category.
Honorable Mention in the 2014 London Book Festival.

Tara Babcock awakes the morn- ing after her 30th birthday with a hangover that could kill an elephant - and the knowledge she is still no closer to achieving closure on her marriage breakup.

Things go from bad to worse when she discovers that, not only is her ex-husband engaged to her cousin - Tash, the woman he left her for - but that Jake is also running for Lord Mayor of Sydney.

Desperate to leave the destructive relationship behind and with nothing to lose, she decides- with encouragement from her three best friends - to follow the dubious advice from a magazine article, *Closure in Seven Easy Steps*.

The Seven Steps to Closure follows Tara on her sometimes disastrous – always hilarious – path to achieve the seemingly impossible.

Follow this link to find out where you can purchase *The Seven Steps to Closure*: https://donnajoyusher-theauthor.com/get-7steps/

Agents Of APE
Book One in
The Alien Private Eye Series

Meet Siccy. She's an arse-kicking, smart-mouthed chick from the Aussie outback. She likes her men complex and her life simple, but all that is about to change. You see Siccy's just woken up from a nap to find that five years have passed.

Now, her fiancé's shacked up with her best friend, and strange creatures are trying to kill her. And if all that wasn't weird enough, the darkly, mysterious Elliot arrives, determined to recruit her as an Alien Private Eye.

But is Elliot who he says he is, and are his claims that the planet is in danger true? Siccy must put her broken heart aside if she is to decipher the truth, thwart the attempts on her life, and go on to save the world.

Visit https://donnajoyusher-theauthor.com/get-ape/ to view purchasing options.

Faery Born
Book One in
The War Faery Trilogy

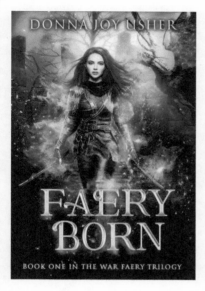

The *War Faery Trilogy* is a fantasy series about Isadora, a witch who finds herself being drawn into the Faery Realm.

It's been thirteen years since the Dark Years ended. Thirteen years since the mad War Faery responsible was imprisoned in stone. Now, with goblin attacks on the rise it seems Galanta, the Goblin Queen, is intent on returning the land to chaos and terror.

Isadora Scrumpleton is trying not to think about the Dark Years. She's just been chosen by her 'familiar', found out she's half faery, and discovered she's dating the second-in-line to the Faery Throne. That's enough for one teenage witch to handle. But when goblins attack her village, Izzy is forced into action, ultimately joining the elite Border Guard and attracting the attention of the Goblin Queen.

As Galanta weaves a web of deceit, Izzy struggles to control her powers. Will she be able to stop the Goblin Queen in time, or will the world be plunged into a dark new reality?

Follow this link to find out where you can buy *Faery Born*: https://donnajoyusher-theauthor.com/get-faery-born/

The *War Faery Trilogy* is available in eBook, print or audible formats.

Made in United States
Troutdale, OR
08/27/2023

12423021R00170